PRAISE FOR GAIL BOWEN AND
THE JOANNE KILBOURN MYSTERIES

"Bowen is one of those rare, magical mystery writers readers love not only for her suspense skills but for her stories' elegance, sense of place and true-to-life form. . . . A master of ramping up suspense"   – *Ottawa Citizen*

"Bowen can confidently place her series beside any other being produced in North America."
                              – Halifax *Chronicle-Herald*

"Gail Bowen's Joanne Kilbourn mysteries are small works of elegance that assume the reader of suspense is after more than blood and guts, that she is looking for the meaning behind a life lived and a life taken."   – *Calgary Herald*

"Bowen has a hard eye for the way human ambition can take advantage of human gullibility."   – *Publishers Weekly*

"Gail Bowen got the recipe right with her series on Joanne Kilbourn."   – *Vancouver Sun*

"What works so well [is Bowen's] sense of place – Regina comes to life – and her ability to inhabit the everyday life of an interesting family with wit and vigour. . . . Gail Bowen continues to be a fine mystery writer, with a protagonist readers can invest in for the long run."
                              – *National Post*

"Gail Bowen is one of Canada's literary treasures."
                              – *Ottawa Citizen*

OTHER JOANNE KILBOURN MYSTERIES
BY GAIL BOWEN

The Nesting Dolls
The Brutal Heart
The Endless Knot
The Last Good Day
The Glass Coffin
Burying Ariel
Verdict in Blood
A Killing Spring
A Colder Kind of Death
Murder at the Mendel (U.S. ed., Love and Murder)
Deadly Appearances

THE WANDERING SOUL MURDERS

A Joanne Kilbourn Mystery

GAIL BOWEN

McClelland & Stewart

Library and Archives Canada Cataloguing in Publication

Bowen, Gail, 1942-
The Wandering Soul Murders : a Joanne Kilbourn mystery / Gail Bowen.

ISBN 978-0-7710-1319-5

I. Title.

PS8553.O8995W35 2011   C813'.54   C2011-900301-5

We acknowledge the financial support of the Government of Canada
through the Book Publishing Industry Development Program and that
of the Government of Ontario through the Ontario Media Development
Corporation's Ontario Book Initiative. We further acknowledge the
support of the Canada Council for the Arts and the Ontario Arts
Council for our publishing program.

Published simultaneously in the United States of America by
McClelland & Stewart Ltd., P.O. Box 1030, Plattsburgh, New York 12901

Library of Congress Control Number: 2011925595

This book was produced using ancient-forest friendly papers.
Typeset in Trump Mediaeval by M&S, Toronto
Printed and bound in Canada

McClelland & Stewart Ltd.
75 Sherbourne Street
Toronto, Ontario
M5A 2P9
www.mcclelland.com

1 2 3 4 5   15 14 13 12 11

With thanks and love to four who made the difference:
my parents, Bert and Doris Bartholomew,
and
my aunt and uncle, Hilda and Gwynne Burke

THE
WANDERING
SOUL
MURDERS

CHAPTER

1

When my daughter, Mieka, found the woman's body in the garbage can behind Old City Hall, she called the police and then she called me. I got there first. The sun was glinting off the glass face of the McCallum-Hill Building as I pulled into the alley behind Mieka's catering shop. It was a little after eight o'clock on a lush Thursday morning in May. It was garbage day, and as I passed the chi-chi pasta place at the corner of Mieka's block, the air smelled heavily of last night's cannelloni warming in the sun.

It wasn't hard to spot the dead woman. Her body was jack-knifed over the edge of the can as if she was reaching inside to retrieve something. But the angle of her body made it apparent that whatever she was looking for wasn't going to be found in this world. Mieka was standing in the shadows behind her. She seemed composed, but when she put her arms around me, I could feel her shaking.

"Come inside," I said.

"I don't want to leave her out here alone," Mieka said, and there was a tone to her voice that made me realize I'd be wise to go along with her.

Without a word, we stepped closer to the garbage can. It was a large one, industrial-size. I looked over the edge. I could see a sweep of black hair and two arms, limp as a doll's, hanging from the armholes of a fluorescent pink tank top. The space Mieka was leasing for her shop was being renovated, and the can was half filled with plaster and construction materials. The plaster underneath the body was stained dark with blood.

I stepped back and looked at Mieka.

"It's the woman who was helping with your cleaning, isn't it?" I asked.

Mieka nodded. "Her name's Bernice Morin." She pointed toward the lower half of the body. "Why would someone do that to her?" she asked.

"I guess they figured killing her didn't debase her enough," I said.

Mieka was gnawing at her lower lip. I felt like gnawing, too, because whoever had murdered Bernice Morin hadn't been content just to take her life. As an extra touch, they had pulled her blue jeans around her ankles, leaving her naked from the waist down. She looked as though she was about to be spanked or sodomized. Sickened at the things we do to one another, I turned away, but not before I saw the tattoo on her left buttock. It was in the shape of a teddy bear.

"My God," I said. "How old was she?"

"Seventeen," said Mieka. "Still teddy bear age."

And then the alley was filled with police, and a seventeen-year-old girl with a teddy bear tattoo became the City of Regina's latest unsolved homicide. I stood and watched as the crime scene people measured and photographed and bagged. And I listened as Mieka told her story to a man who had the sad basset eyes of the actor Donald Sutherland and who introduced himself as Inspector Tom Zaba.

Mieka's story wasn't much. Bernice Morin had been

cleaning for her under the city's fine-option program. It was a way people without money could work off unpaid fines for traffic tickets or minor misdemeanours. The building in which Mieka was leasing space was city property, so she had been eligible to get someone from the program. Mieka told the inspector that Bernice Morin had been working at the shop for a week. No one had visited her, and there had been no phone calls that Mieka knew about. Bernice hadn't appeared to be upset or frightened about anything, but Mieka said they hadn't spent much time together. She had been in and out, dealing with glaziers and carpenters, and Bernice wasn't much of a talker.

When the inspector asked her when she had last seen Bernice Morin alive, Mieka's jaw clenched. "Yesterday," she said, "about four-thirty. My fiancé's mother brought his grandfather by to take me out to their golf club to arrange for our wedding reception. I told Bernice I was coming back, but then Lorraine, my fiancé's mother, decided we should all stay out at the club for dinner. If I'd come back . . ." Mieka's voice trailed off. She was looking down at her hands as if she'd never seen them before.

Inspector Zaba took a step toward her. "Keep your focus, Miss Kilbourn. You were at the country club. Did you call Bernice Morin to tell her you'd be delayed?"

Mieka seemed wholly absorbed in her fingers, but her voice was strong. "I called a little before six and asked Bernice if she'd mind locking up when she left."

"And your premises were locked when you arrived this morning at . . . ?"

"At around seven-thirty. I'm an early riser. And, no, the shop wasn't locked. The front door was closed, but the dead-bolt wasn't on, and the back door, the one that opens onto the alley, was open. There was a pigeon flying around in the store. And there were bird droppings on the counter."

Inspector Zaba looked at Mieka expectantly.

Mieka shrugged. "I chased the pigeon around for a while until it finally flew out, then I cleaned up and I brought the dirty rags out here to the garbage. That's when I found Bernice. I went inside and phoned you and then I called my mother."

A female constable came outside and told Inspector Zaba that there was a phone call for Mieka. He nodded and told Mieka she could take it, but when she went into the building, he followed her.

I stayed behind, and that's when I heard two of the younger cops talking. One of them apparently knew Bernice pretty well.

"She was a veteran," he said. "On the streets for as long as I was in vice, and that was three years. She was from up north; she used to be one of that punk Darren Wolfe's girls."

The other man looked at him. "Another Little Flower homicide?"

"Looks like," said the first cop. "The bare bum's right. The face didn't seem mutilated, but maybe they'll pick up something downtown."

The young cops moved over to the garbage can and started bagging hunks of bloody plaster. They didn't seem to feel like talking any more. I didn't blame them.

When Mieka came out, it was apparent that the brutal reality of the murder had hit her. Her skin was waxy, covered with a light sheen of sweat. I didn't like the way she looked, and apparently Inspector Zaba didn't, either.

He came over to me and lowered his voice to a rasp. "I think we know what we've got here, Mrs. Kilbourn, and your daughter looks like she's had enough. Get her out of here. We've got all we need from her for the moment."

Grateful, I started to walk away, but I couldn't leave without asking. "What do you think you've got?" I said.

Inspector Tom Zaba had a face that would have been transformed by a smile, but I had the sense he didn't smile often.

"An object lesson," he said. "In the past year, we've had four of these murders." He looked thoughtfully at Bernice Morin's body and then at me. When he spoke, his voice was patient, the voice of a teacher explaining a situation to an unpromising student. "We've got some common denominators in these cases, Mrs. Kilbourn. One, all the victims were hustlers who'd gone independent. Two, all the girls walked out on pimps who don't believe in free enterprise. Three, the faces of all the victims were mutilated. Four, all the dead girls were found with the lower halves of their bodies exposed." He raised his eyebrows. "You don't have to be a shrink or a cop to get the message, do you?"

I looked at Bernice Morin's body. Her legs were strong and slender. She must have been a woman who moved with grace. I felt a coldness in the pit of my stomach.

"No," I said, "you don't have to be a shrink or a cop to get the message."

Victoria Park looks like every other inner-city park in every other small city in Canada: a large and handsome memorial to the war dead surrounded by a square block of hard-tracked grass with benches where people can sit and look at statues of politicians or at flower beds planted with petunias and marigolds, the cheap and the hardy, downtown survivors.

Mieka and I sat on a bench in front of Sir John A. Macdonald. It was a little after nine, and we had the park pretty much to ourselves. In three hours, the Mr. Tube Steak vendors would be filling the air with the smell of steaming wieners and sauerkraut, and the workers would spill out of the offices around Victoria Park and sit on the grass in their short-sleeved shirts and pastel spring dresses and turn their pale spring faces to the sun. But that was in the future. The only people in the park now were the sad ones with trembling hands and desperate eyes who had nowhere else to go.

And us. We sat side by side, not saying anything for a few minutes, then Mieka started to talk. Her voice was high and strained. "I only ever really talked to her once, Mummy, and it was here. One morning we came over here so Bernice could have a smoke. We talked about her tattoos. She was so proud of them. She had a snake that curled around here." Mieka traced a circle around the firm flesh of her upper arm. "Bernice was wearing a tank top that day, and she caught me staring at the snake. I was embarrassed, so I mumbled something complimentary. Then she just opened up. Told me she'd gotten the snake done down in Montana, and she thought it was so hot, she'd had a rose done on the other arm. She said all the people she hung with thought the snake and the rose were the best, but that was because they hadn't seen her private tattoo.

"Then she did something strange. We were sitting over there by the swings. Bernice looked around to make sure we were alone, then she turned away from me and hiked up her tank top. On her back was a picture of unicorns dancing.

"I knew it was an honour that she was showing me the tattoo, and I knew I should say something, but I just choked. Finally, Bernice pulled her shirt back down and laughed. 'Knocked you out, eh?' she said. Then she said she wanted me to see her back so I'd know she wasn't just somebody who did cleaning.

"I didn't mean to ignore her, Mum. You know I'd never be mean deliberately, but I guess I was just so busy I didn't pay much attention to her . . ."

I put my arm around my daughter's shoulder and pulled

her toward me. "It's okay, Miek," I said. "It's okay." But I knew it wasn't, and so did Mieka.

Her eyes were filled with sadness. "I haven't told you about the unicorns. Bernice dreamed about them one night after her boyfriend beat her up. The next morning she made the drawing, then she took the bus up north to a tattoo artist she knew who could do the design right. She said it took three hours and it just about killed her, especially the parts on her shoulder blades, but she said the unicorns were so beautiful they were worth it."

"Let's go home, baby," I said.

She shook me off. "Do you know what she told me, Mummy? She said she liked unicorns because they were the only animal that refused to go on the ark with Noah, and that's why they're extinct. She said her boyfriend told her it was because they were so dumb, but Bernice said she thought it was because they were too proud to get intimidated." Mieka's face was crumpling in pain. "That's what she said, Mummy. Unicorns died out because they were too proud to get intimidated."

Finally the tears came, and I took my daughter home. She slept most of the morning, but when I came back after picking up my youngest child, Taylor, from nursery school, Mieka was sitting at the kitchen table and there was a plate of sandwiches in front of her.

"Peanut butter and jelly for Taylor and salmon for us," Mieka said. She bent down and gave Taylor a quick hug. "Sound good to you, kiddo?"

Taylor beamed. "Look," she said, "I made you something, too. I did it at school." It was a painting. In the centre of the page, a baby lamb nuzzled its mother and a chick cracked the top of an egg. The rest of the page was alive with red tulips. They were everywhere: bursting through the grass on

the ground and the clouds in the sky. A corona of them shot
out in a halo of red around the yellow sun. On the top, in
the careful printing of the nursery school teacher, were the
words "NEW LIFE."

I tapped the words with my fingertip. "Life will go on, you
know," I said, looking at Mieka.

She smiled and said quietly, "I know. It's just hard to think
that it won't go on for Bernice. Seventeen is too young."

"Too young for what?" asked Taylor.

"Too young to miss the spring," Mieka said, turning away.
"Now, come on, T., what's the drink of choice with peanut
butter and jelly?"

After lunch, Mieka said she had some errands she should
do, and she'd feel better if she was busy. Taylor and I drove
to the nursery to buy bedding plants. It felt good to stand in
the sunshine, picking up boxes of new plants, smelling
damp earth and looking at fresh green shoots. As we drove
home, Taylor was still curling her tongue around the
names: sugar daddies, double mixed pinks, sweet rocket,
bachelor's-button, black-eyed Susans. By the time we
pulled into the driveway her lids were heavy and she came
in, curled up on the couch and fell asleep. I covered her
with a blanket, poured a cup of coffee and dialled the
number of a friend of mine from the old days before my
husband died.

Jill Osiowy was director of news at NationTV now, but
when I met her, in 1971, she'd just been hired as a press
officer by our provincial government. It was her first job, and
she was very young. We were all young. My husband was
twenty-eight when he was elected to the House that year,
and when we formed the government, he became the
youngest attorney general in the country.

In those days, Jill's hair was an explosion of shoulder-length red curls, and she wore Earth shoes and hand-embroidered denim work shirts. She was smart and earnest, and her face shone with the faith that she could change the future. By the time we lost in 1982, Jill's hair was sleek as the silk shirts and meticulously tailored suits she bought in Toronto twice a year; she was still smart and she was still earnest, but she'd had some bruising encounters with political realities, and the glow had dimmed a little.

She had used the first years after the government changed to go back to school. She got two graduate degrees in journalism, taught for a while at Ryerson in Toronto, then came back to Regina and her first love, TV news.

That afternoon, when she heard my voice, Jill gave a throaty whoop. "Well, la-di-da, you're back in town. I'd heard rumours but since you never actually phoned me, I didn't want to believe them."

"Believe them," I said. "And as susceptible to guilt as I am, you can't guilt me on this because we've only been back in Regina two weeks. We're not even unpacked yet."

"Okay," she said, "I'll come over and help you unpack. That'll guilt you."

"Right now?" I asked.

"Sure. I'm just poring over our anemic budget trying to find some money that didn't get spent. Depressing work for the first five-star day we've had this month."

"Come over then. It'd be great to see you. But listen, I was calling for another reason, too. Have you heard anything about a case called the Little Flower murders?"

Jill whistled, "I've heard a lot. One of our investigative units is putting together a feature on it. I can bring over some of their tapes if you like." She was quiet for a beat. "What's your interest in this, Jo?"

"I'll tell you when you get here. Listen, I bought a new house. Same neighbourhood as I lived in before I moved to

Saskatoon, but over on Regina Avenue." I gave her the address. "Twenty minutes?"

"Fifteen," she said. "I've been cooped up here long enough. I'm starting to wilt."

When I saw her coming up the front walk, she didn't look like a woman who was wilting. She looked sensational, and I was conscious of the fact that I hadn't changed since I'd grabbed my blue jeans and an old Mets T-shirt out of the clean laundry when Mieka had called that morning. Jill's red hair was cut in a short bob, and she was wearing an orangey-gold T-shirt, an oversize unbleached cotton jacket, short in the front and long in the back, and matching pants. On the lapel of her jacket she had pinned a brilliant silk sunflower.

"You look like a van Gogh picnic," I said, hugging her. "Where did you get that outfit?"

"Value Village," she said. "It's all second-hand."

"How come when I wear Value Village it looks like Value Village?"

"Because you're too conservative, Jo. You've got to force yourself to walk by the polyester pantsuits." She stepped past me into the front hall and looked around. "My God, this isn't a polyester pantsuit kind of house. You must be doing all right."

"Well, I am doing all right," I said, "but not this all right. Come on, let me give you the grand tour, and I'll tell you about it."

Even after two weeks, I felt a thrill when I walked around our new home. It was a beautiful house, thirty years old, solid, with big sunny rooms and lots of Laura Ashley wallpaper and oak floors and gleaming woodwork. I loved being a tour guide and Jill was a wonderful companion: enthusiastic, flattering and funny. When we walked out in the backyard and she saw the pool glittering in the sun, she said, "This really is sublime." Then our dogs came out of the house and ran down the hill. Sadie, the collie, stopped dead at the edge of the pool, but Rose, the golden retriever, jumped in and began doing laps.

"Not so sublime," I said.

Jill grimaced. "Does that happen often?"

"She's getting used to it," I said. "We're down to about fourteen times a day."

"This is why I have cats," Jill said.

"Lou and Murray are still alive?" I said, surprised.

"They're planning their joint birthday celebration even as we speak," Jill said. "They'll be thirteen July 29."

"Come on," I said, "let's go in and get a beer and you can tell me all about it. Are cat years the same as dog years? Are Lou and Murray really going to be ninety, or just thirteen?"

"You're mocking us," Jill said, "so I'm not going to tell you. Let's hear your family's news."

We went into the kitchen. Jill found a couple of beer glasses while I opened the beer.

"You did hear, didn't you," I said, "that I've adopted a little girl? Her name is Taylor, and she's five. She was my friend Sally Love's daughter."

Jill's eyes looked sad. "I heard about Sally, of course. That was such a tragedy."

"Yeah," I said. "I don't think any of us are over it yet. Anyway, there was no one to take Taylor, so I did. It seems to be working out. The kids are really good with her, and I think Taylor's beginning to feel that we're her family."

"She's lucky to have you," Jill said. "Not every kid gets Gaia, the Earth Mother."

"Well, thanks," I said, "I think."

We brought out two bottles of Great West and sat at the picnic table and watched Rose do her patient laps. It was a perfect day, still and sunny and warm. Jill turned to me. "This is what my mother and her friends used to do when I was growing up," she said. "Twenty-fourth of May weekend they'd hit the backyards and start working on their tans. My mother used to call it her summer project."

"Do you want to go back to that?" I asked.

"Lord, no," she said. "Now tell me about the house."

"Actually it was Sally's lawyer's idea. When I was making the arrangements to adopt Taylor, he asked me if I was going to have to renovate my old house for an extra child. In fact, I'd planned to. Nothing very elaborate, but Taylor's inherited her mother's talent for making art."

"Not a bad inheritance," Jill said.

"Not bad at all. It's amazing to see. You read about gifted children, but to actually live with a little kid who has this incredible talent is something else again. Anyway, I told Sally's lawyer I wanted to add on a room where Taylor could paint. He just about patted me on the head. 'Good, good,' he said, 'we mustn't ignore the fact that in cases like these the concept of life expectations comes into play.' "

Jill shook her head. "Ugh, lawyer talk. What are life expectations?"

"According to this guy it's a term the law uses to describe what Taylor could have expected her life to be like given her parents' earning power and position in the community. Sally and Stuart Lachlan were both wealthy people – so the lawyer said Taylor could have reasonably expected to grow up with pretty much everything she wanted."

"I don't like the sound of that," Jill said thoughtfully.

"Neither did I," I said, "but in this particular case it simply meant investing a little money from Taylor's trust fund in the place she was going to live. At first I was going to put it toward the new addition, but then this house came on the market. I'd gotten a pretty good advance for that biography I wrote about Andy Boychuk, and you know what a slump real estate's in here. With what I got for our old house and the advance, this place really didn't cost much more than the renovations would have."

"And this is so spiffy," Jill said.

"Right," I said, "and this is so spiffy. Can I get you another beer?"

"No, I've got a meeting at four o'clock with the vice-president of finance. He's coming out from head office, and I need to smell hard-working and underfunded." She looked at her watch. "If we're going to look at the Little Flower tape, we'd better do it now. You never did tell me why you're interested."

I tried to keep the emotion out of my voice. "This morning Mieka found a body in the garbage can outside the place she's going to have her catering business. It was a woman who had done some cleaning for her – actually it was a girl, seventeen. I overheard one of the cops say it looked like another Little Flower murder."

Jill's body was tense with interest. "Was the face mutilated?"

"I couldn't see her face," I said. "But whoever killed her had pulled her slacks and panties down around her ankles."

"Bastard." Jill spit the word into the fine May afternoon.

Her face was ashen as we walked into the house. Neither of us said a word as Jill put the tape in the VCR and the first pictures filled the screen. They were sickening. Reflexively, I closed my eyes. When I opened them, the images on the screen were even worse. The camera had pulled in for a tight shot of the inside of a commercial garbage bin. There were two girls lying on some garbage in the bin. They looked as if they had been folded in two and dropped in. Both girls were naked from the waist down, and each of them had long hair that fell in a dark pillow behind her head. They would have looked like children hiding if it weren't for their unnatural stillness and for the hideous distortion violence had made of their faces. The features were unrecognizable; eyes, nose and lips had run together into a charred, melted mass.

Beside me, Jill said quietly, "Their names were Debbie and Donna Lavallee. They were twins."

The camera panned the grey sky and dirty snow of a city alley in late winter. Then it focused on the next victim. Her pants had been removed, too. She was splayed over the rim of an oil can so that the edge hit her vaginal area.

"Michele Macdonald," Jill said. "Be grateful you can't see her face."

The dirty snow and grey skies were gone in the next pictures. It was spring, and the sky was bright as the camera zoomed in on the industrial garbage can. This girl's body was leaning into the can the way Bernice Morin's had been. When the camera positioned itself over her shoulder and focused down, I could see that she'd worn her blonde hair in a ponytail.

"Two years ago she was a cheerleader at Holy Name," Jill said. "Her name was Cindy Duchek."

I sat there stunned. I felt as if I had been kicked in the stomach. Finally, I said, "Where did the name Little Flower murders come from?"

"The bodies of the girls in that first picture, the Lavallee twins, were found behind Little Flower Church."

"Kind of a variation on the baby left on the cathedral doorstep," I said.

Jill looked at me hard. "Are you all right?"

"I don't know," I said. "It's the worst thing I've ever seen. How old were they?"

"They were all fifteen."

I thought of Mieka at fifteen. The biggest problems in her life had been the shape of her nose and her algebra marks. "How does it happen?" I said. "How does a young girl get to the point where life on the street is an option?"

Jill looked weary. "You know, Jo, the street isn't a last resort for these kids. For a lot of them, it's a step up. When they meet that guy with the Camaro and he tells them he loves them and promises to take care of them, it must sound like they've died and gone to heaven."

"And the next step is . . ."

"And the next step is three-inch heels, fuck-me pants and their own little corner on Broad Street." Jill's voice was bitter. "And it just keeps getting better. I'm sorry, Jo. This Little Flower thing really gets to me. No one seems to care about those girls. I don't mean the cops aren't investigating. They are. But there hasn't exactly been a public outcry to find the killers."

"Because the girls are prostitutes?" I asked.

"Because people think they're garbage," Jill said. "And nice people are always relieved when someone else takes out the garbage. What was that term your lawyer friend came up with? Life expectations? Well, the life expectations for these girls are zero. Zip. Nothing. And once their lives kick into high gear, the odds start going down."

She stood up, and the contrast between the bright sunflower on her jacket and the despair in her eyes was pretty hard to take.

We were silent as we walked through the house. At the front door Jill turned to me. "I'm glad you're back in town, Jo. Hey, tell Mieka congratulations for me, would you? I saw her engagement announcement in the paper. I hope what happened this morning doesn't cast too long a shadow on all the happy times ahead."

"I hope you get your wish," I said.

But she didn't.

CHAPTER

2

Mieka was too quiet during dinner. After we'd put the dishes in the dishwasher, she started down the hall to her room. I didn't want her to be alone, and I went after her.

"Why don't we go out on the deck and watch the kids for a while?" I said. "Your brother and Camilo are showing Taylor how to take care of baseball equipment. We've already missed how to sand a bat."

Mieka shook her head. "Taylor will be the hottest rookie in Little League," she said, as she followed me out the back door. Angus and his friend Camilo were kneeling on the deck oiling their gloves. Taylor was between them, watching intently.

I touched Angus on the shoulder. "Maybe if you didn't use quite so much Vaseline, you'd get over your fielding problems," I said. He looked up at me, pained, and Taylor moved a little closer to him. It seemed like a good sign that she was already on his side, and I wasn't surprised when she decided to go to 7-Eleven with the boys instead of staying home with Mieka and me.

After they left, I turned to Mieka. "Feel like taking the dogs for a walk?" I asked.

"Your solution for everything," she said. "A shower or a walk. And I'm already clean. Sure, let's go."

It was a beautiful evening, and we followed the bicycle path all the way out to Mieka's old high school on Royal Road. As we walked around the grounds, we could hear the lazy whoosh of the sprinklers watering the new geraniums and the sounds of kids playing Frisbee.

Bernice Morin's death and the tapes of the Little Flower victims were fresh wounds, but the problem that dogged me as we walked around the old high school was five months old.

That morning when Mieka had called and asked me to come down to the shop was the first time she had turned to me since January. The rupture had begun when she dropped out of school in Saskatoon and used the fund her father and I had set up for university to buy a catering business called Judgements. Despite my predictions, Judgements had caught on like wildfire, and when the chance came to open a sister business in Regina, Mieka hadn't missed a beat. She drew up estimates on how much it would cost to lease and renovate space in Old City Hall, then she went to her fiancé's mother, Lorraine Harris, and borrowed the money. It wasn't until the papers were signed that she told me what she'd done. I'd been furious: furious at Mieka for getting in over her head and furious at Lorraine Harris for letting her get in over her head. And something else: I was jealous, jealous that Mieka had gone to Greg's mother rather than coming to me.

We loved each other too much to risk a no-holds-barred confrontation, but there had been some troubled weeks. Then, when we came back to Regina, I'd asked Mieka to move home. It seemed like a good idea all around. With two new businesses and a September wedding, Mieka's life was pressing in on her. I thought being with me and the kids and having the details of day-to-day living taken care of would help her deal with the demands of the summer. For me, of course, it meant a chance to get our relationship back to the old closeness. The perfect solution to everybody's problems. But, like a lot of perfect solutions, this one hadn't worked.

Mieka had changed. She was a woman and, in many respects, a stranger. In my more honest moments, I knew it was wrong to want her to be the sweet, pliable girl she had been at eighteen. Twenty times a day, I repeated C.P. Snow's line that the love between a parent and a child is the only love that must grow toward separation. Every morning I woke up determined to be open and reasonable, and every night I went to bed knowing I had been neither. My only justification was that I believed I was right. In my heart, I felt my daughter had chosen the wrong path.

That night, as I looked at Mieka's profile, so familiar and so dear, somehow being right didn't seem important any more.

As if she had read my mind, Mieka turned. "Was John Lennon the one who said, 'There's nothing like death to put life in perspective'?"

I smiled at her. "I don't know, but whoever said it, it's a good thought."

Her eyes filled with tears. "I'm sorry things have been bad between us, Mummy."

That was when I started to cry. "Oh, Miek, I'm sorry, too. All I ever wanted was what was best for you."

Mieka reached in her pocket, pulled out a Kleenex and handed it to me. "Peace offering," she said. Then she smiled. "Do you remember that time Peter decided to take up wrestling?"

"Some of my darkest hours as a mother."

"But you let him. I remember you went to all his matches."

"Including the one where your brother got knocked unconscious. I'm still proud of the fact that I didn't jump in the ring that night and cradle him in my arms."

Mieka took my hand. "That must have been hard for you. You're not exactly deficient in the motherly instincts department, you know."

I turned to look at her. "I take it you'd like me to work on suppressing those instincts for a while."

"Yeah, Mum, I would." Her voice was strong and determined. "I want my chance. I know I may get flattened, but I have to try."

I gave her hand a squeeze. "One good thing about me," I said, "I always know when I'm licked."

Mieka smiled. "Don't think of it as being licked. Think of it as accepting the inevitable gracefully."

"Same thing, eh?" I said.

Her smile grew broader. "Oh, yeah," she said, "it's the same thing, but this way you get to look like a good guy."

We walked home arm in arm, like chums in a 1940s movie, and as we settled into our old pattern of comfortable, aimless talk, I was filled with gratitude.

When Mieka hesitated at the back gate of our yard, my first thought was that she wanted to tell me she was grateful, too. But as I watched her square her shoulders and take a deep breath, I knew that whatever was coming was not happy talk. When there was bad news, Mieka never wasted time in preamble.

"Christy Sinclair came into Judgements yesterday," she said. "I wasn't going to mention it because I knew it would upset you, but considering everything else that's happened . . ." She shrugged her shoulders.

"What did she want?" I asked.

"She wanted to know where Peter was."

"Did you tell her?"

"Yes, I did," Mieka said. "She made it sound so urgent, and there were other people there. Bernice, and Greg's mother, and poor Blaine was waiting outside in the car. It just seemed easier to tell her."

"Damn," I said, "I'd hoped Christy was out of your brother's life – out of all our lives."

"Maybe she is," Mieka said wearily. "Christy has always been unpredictable."

"I wish that's all she was," I said. "Her problem's more serious than that. I think it's a pathology, and it scares me."

Mieka was silent. Suddenly the magic had gone from the evening. The light faded, the wind came up, and someone on a bicycle yelled at the dogs. If you believed in omens, the signs accompanying Christy Sinclair's re-entry into our lives didn't bode well.

When Peter had begun dating her before Christmas, we had all been ecstatic. He was nineteen years old and painfully shy. There had never been a girlfriend. Christy was exuberant and outgoing – just the ticket, it seemed. She was his biology lab instructor, and when it turned out that she was not twenty-one, as she had told Pete at first, but twenty-five, I took a deep breath and tried not to let it worry me. But as the winter wore on, other things started to.

Christy's lie about her age had not been an aberration. She lied about everything: where she'd eaten lunch; the names of the people with whom she had spent the weekend; the way her superiors in the biology department assessed her work performance. That winter I had been teaching political science at the university where Christy was working. She must have known the lies she told about her daily life would come to light, but it didn't seem to alarm her. In an odd way, it seemed to make her more reckless. As the winter wore on, her lies became more transparent, more vulnerable to disclosure. It was a frightening thing to witness.

There was another thing. I had been touched at first by how much Christy liked us, but it began to appear that her need to be part of our family was obsessive. She wanted to be at our house all the time, and when she was there, she wanted to be with me. She was an educated and capable woman, but she followed me around with the dogged determination of a tired child. I tried to understand, to sympathize with whatever privation had brought about this immense need, but the truth was Christy Sinclair got under my skin. When I was with her, I itched to get away; when I got away, I felt guilty because I knew how much being with me mattered to her.

As the winter wore on, it became clear that I wasn't the only one Christy was making miserable. She was crowding Peter, too. Night after night, I could hear her, pressing him for a permanent commitment. Peter was, in many ways, a very young nineteen-year-old. I was almost certain that Christy was the first woman with whom he'd been intimate. He was an innocent kid. My husband used to say that innocence is just a step away from crippling stupidity. He was warning me, not Peter, but my son's unquestioning acceptance of people made him vulnerable, too. Peter wasn't stupid, but it wouldn't have taken much for Christy to convince him that a sexual relationship needed to be legitimized.

By Easter, Christy seemed to be a permanent part of our lives; she was the problem without a solution. Then one day Peter came home and told me he had taken a job at a vet clinic in Swift Current until the fall semester started. It seemed too good to be true.

"What about Christy?" I asked.

"It's over," he said, and he'd looked so miserable that I hadn't pressed the matter. I never did find out what had happened between them. I didn't care. It was finished, and I was grateful. These days when Pete called to talk he sounded relaxed and hopeful. Now, just a little over a month after he'd set us free, it seemed as if we might become entangled again.

"Stay away, Christy," I said to the warm spring night. "Just please stay away."

When I walked into the house, the phone was ringing. The old ones used to say that if you mentioned the name of an enemy, you conjured him up. Christy Sinclair wasn't my enemy, but when I heard her low, husky voice on the phone, I felt a superstitious chill. If I hadn't said her name aloud, perhaps she wouldn't have materialized.

As always, she rushed in headlong. "Oh, Jo, it's wonderful to hear your voice again. Guess what? Pete and I are back together."

I held my breath. There was still the chance that she was lying, still the possibility that this was just another case where Christy had crossed the line between what she wanted and what was true. But when she spoke again, I knew she hadn't crossed the line.

"Pete says Greg's family is throwing a big engagement party at their cottage, Friday – a kickoff for the Victoria Day weekend. He suggested that I ride down with you and the kids. He won't be able to get there from Swift Current till around seven. Jo, are you still there? Is that all right with you?"

I felt numb. It was all beginning again.

"Yes," I said, "if that's what Pete wants, it's fine with me."

"Great," she said. "What time should I come over?"

"Around four, I guess. I thought we'd leave as soon as Angus got back from school."

"Great. Four o'clock tomorrow. I'm counting the minutes."

I walked down the hall to Mieka's room and knocked on the door. She was sitting on her bed reading a bride's magazine, and when she saw me, she laughed and hid the magazine behind her back.

"My name is Ditzi with an *i*," she said in the singsong cadence of a TV mall stomper. "Oh, Mum, I can't believe I'm reading this. But since I am, what do you think of that one?" She pointed to a dress that was all ruffles and lace. "It has a hoop sewn into the skirt."

"I guess it would be all right if you were marrying Rhett Butler," I said, sitting down next to her. "Whatever would you do with something like that afterwards?"

Mieka raised an eyebrow. "Frankly, my dear," she said, "I wouldn't give a damn."

It was good to see her laugh, but as I told her about Christy's phone call, her face fell.

"Poor Peter. What are we going to do, Mum?"

"Nothing," I said. "Remember what you said about the wrestling? It's his life. We'll be nice to Christy and hope for the best."

But at four o'clock the next day, as I watched Christy Sinclair get out of her car, I knew that being nice and hoping for the best were going to be hard.

Even her red Volkswagen convertible brought back memories. At the end of her relationship with Peter, I had felt my heart sink every time the Volks had pulled into our driveway. But I tried to be positive. Christy looked great. She always did. She wasn't a beautiful woman, but she had a lively androgynous charm – slim hips, flat chest, dark curly hair cut boy short. And she always dressed the part. Christy was estranged from her family, but she said they always made sure she had the best of everything. Today, for a trip to the country she looked like she'd stepped out of an L.L. Bean ad: sneakers, white cotton overalls and a blue-and-white striped shirt. As soon as she saw me standing in the doorway, she ran up and threw her arms around me. She smelled good, of cotton and English soap and sunshine.

"I've missed this family," she said, her voice breaking. Then she stood back and looked at me. "And I've missed you most of all, Jo." She smiled.

It was hard not to respond to that smile. Christy's best feature was her mouth; it was large, mobile, expressive. Theodore Roethke wrote a poem where he talks about a young girl's sidelong pickerel smile; Christy Sinclair's smile was like that – whimsical, sly and knowing.

"We had some good times," I said. It seemed a neutral enough statement.

"Right," she said, and this time there was no mistaking the mocking line of her mouth. "Good times, Jo." She reached over and picked up a suitcase and threw it into the trunk of my car. "And we're going to have more."

Her words were defiant, but there was a vulnerability in her voice that hadn't been there before. She sounded almost desperate, and I was grateful when the kids came barrelling out of the house. In the flurry of bags being stowed in the car and the greetings and last-minute instructions to the girl next door who was going to take care of the dogs, I didn't have to weigh the words I would say to Christy.

Apparently, though, she'd already thought of what she wanted to say to me. As the solid homes of College Avenue gave way to the strip malls and fast-food restaurants of Park Street, Christy turned to me.

"What's the date of Mieka's wedding?" she asked.

"It's the Saturday of Labour Day weekend."

"Maybe Peter and I can make it a double wedding," Christy said, and I felt a chill.

From the back seat Angus's voice broke with adolescent exasperation. "Pete's just a kid. He can't get married."

Christy shrugged and smiled her knowing smile, but Taylor had heard a word that interested her. "Samantha at my school says that when her sister got married, their poodle wore a wedding suit and carried the rings down the aisle on a little pillow."

Angus snorted. "Great idea, T. Can you imagine our dogs in a church?"

"They could have dresses," Taylor said resolutely, "dresses for a wedding."

Angus was mollifying. "Well, yeah, maybe if they had dresses, it would be okay." Then he exploded in laughter again.

Between the dogs in their bridesmaids' dresses and Christy's suggestion about a double wedding, there didn't seem to be much left to say. As we pulled onto the Trans-Canada east of the city, we settled into a silence that if it wasn't companionable was at least endurable.

It had been a wet spring. The fields were green with the new crop, and the sloughs were filled with water. On that gentle afternoon, the drive to the Qu'Appelle Valley was a pretty one, and as we travelled along the ribbon-flat highway, I was soothed into daydreaming. Just before Edenwold, the air outside the car was split with a high-pitched whooping.

Beside me, Christy was excited. "Oh, Jo, look over there in that field – those are tundra swans. You have to pull over to let the kids see."

To the left was a slough, and it was white with birds. There must have been thousands of them. The air was alive with their mournful cries and the beating of their powerful wings.

I pulled over on the shoulder, and Christy and I and the kids ran over and doubled back along the fence.

Taylor was tagging along behind Christy. "Where are they going?" Taylor shouted, raising her voice so she could be heard above the racket.

"The Arctic Circle," Christy shouted back, and she turned and took Taylor's hand. "They spend the winter in Texas and they fly north for the summer. They're a little off their migration path."

Taylor stopped in her tracks. "If they're lost, how will they find their way?"

In the brilliant May sunshine Christy looked young and defenceless. "Instinct," she said, "and luck. If they're smart and they're lucky, they'll make it."

I liked her better in that moment than I had in weeks. As she stood by the fence and watched that prairie slough filled with swans, it seemed as if the mask had dropped and the woman who lived behind that complex repertory of roles Christy played had revealed herself. I had said to Mieka that all we could do was wait and hope for the best. Maybe there really was a best. I was reluctant to make the moment end.

"I guess we'd better go," I said finally. "They're expecting us for supper."

As we passed Balgonie, I noticed that it was close to five o'clock, and I reached over and switched on the car radio for the news. Bernice Morin's murder was the lead story. The announcer's voice was young, nasal and relentlessly upbeat. "Regina police announced a possible break in the Bernice Morin case. A witness has come forward with the information that at seven-thirty on the night of the murder, he heard a cry in the alley behind Old City Hall. When he looked down the alley, he saw a jogger running south. The jogger is described as five feet seven, slender, wearing grey sweatpants and a hooded grey sweatshirt. Police ask that anyone having –"

Beside me, Christy reached over and savagely turned the radio off.

I was surprised that she wasn't interested. "You met her," I said. "Mieka said she was in the store Tuesday afternoon when you came in."

I noticed a tightening in the muscles of Christy's neck. She didn't say anything.

"She was so young," I said. "She had all her life ahead of her."

"She was just a hooker," Christy said coldly.

I was so angry I wanted to shake her, but she cut me off. She turned her back to me and stayed that way, looking out the window of the passenger seat, till we got to the Harrises. I could hear her breathing, tense and unhappy, but she didn't say a word. As far as I was concerned, that was fine. An hour after she'd come back into our lives, I'd already had enough of Christy Sinclair.

By the time the highway started its slow descent into the Qu'Appelle Valley I'd decided that letting my son get the wind knocked out of him in the wrestling ring was one matter; standing by while he entered into a serious relationship with a cruel and angry young woman was another. As soon as I had a chance, I was going to talk to Peter about Christy.

Once I'd made the decision I felt better; when I saw the rolling hills of the Qu'Appelle I felt better yet. I had been to the valley a thousand times, but it had never lost its power to quicken my pulse. We turned off the highway and drove up the narrow winding roads until we passed a sign that said we were entering Standing Buffalo Indian Reserve. Below, Echo Lake glittered, and on the other side of the water, the hills rose green with spring.

It wasn't long till we drove out of reserve land, and the ubiquitous signs of cottage country thrust themselves up along the road: "Heart's Eze," "The Pines," "Dunrovin." Through the trees I could see the bright outlines of the cottages hugging the hills overlooking the lake. At the crest of the highest hill we came to a discreet cedar sign that said, "Eden."

"This is it," I said to the kids. "We are about to enter the Garden of Eden. And you guys always say I never take you anywhere."

Hedges of caragana protected what was behind from public view. We drove through the gate and along a road narrowed by bushes and wildflowers. At the turn, we came to a clearing; below was the summer cottage of the family of the late Alisdair Harris.

Except it wasn't a cottage; it was a country home, a handsome old dowager of a house of gleaming white clapboard with verandas on both storeys and gingerbread trim. At the side of the house, a pool, its water an improbable turquoise, shimmered in the late afternoon sun. White wrought-iron chairs and tables, already set for dinner, ringed the manicured green of the lawn around the pool.

The air smelled of fresh-cut grass, and in the distance I could hear the song of the valley's birds. It really was Eden, or as close to Eden as I expected to come on this side of the grave.

"No snakes in this paradise," I said.

"Good," said Taylor. "I'm scared of snakes."

"I'm not," said Angus. "Anyway, the only kind of snakes around here are garter snakes, and they never hurt anybody. You've got nothing to worry about, T."

But Angus was wrong, and I was wrong, too. In that serene and perfect world, there was a serpent waiting. Before the night was over, it would glide silently across our lives, leaving behind its dark gifts of death and evil, changing us all forever.

CHAPTER

3

When he saw that there was a tennis court behind the house, Angus rolled down his window.

"Look out, Toto, we're not in Kansas any more," he said.

Beside him, Taylor laughed appreciatively. I would have bet my last dollar she'd never heard of the Wizard of Oz, but it didn't matter. Angus was her brother now, and she was determined to be his best audience.

Greg and Mieka had driven out to the lake earlier in the day, and as soon as we pulled up, Mieka came running out of the house to greet us. She hugged me, scooped up Taylor for a kiss, and gave her brother's shoulders a squeeze. Then she turned to Christy, who was standing apart from us in the driveway.

"You're sharing a room with me," she said. "Just let me grab some of my family's twenty thousand bags and I'll show you where you can freshen up."

With Mieka's welcome, some of the misery seemed to leave Christy's face, and I could feel my body relax. When Mieka was around, life had a way of working out, and I smiled gratefully at her.

She grinned. "Dinner's at six-thirty, you guys – my mother-in-law-to-be is a stickler for punctuality."

We carried our bags into the house, and Christy disappeared upstairs with Mieka. Taylor and I were sharing a room, and Angus was in what Mieka had described as the male wing of the house.

"My new family believes in propriety," Mieka had said, deadpan. "Men on one side, women on the other; don't embarrass me with any midnight creeping."

I closed the door and looked gratefully around our room. It had a spectacular view of the hills and the lake. Everything in it was the palest shade of pink.

"Look," I said to Taylor, "your favourite colour."

"Do you think Mieka picked the pink room for me?"

"Absolutely," I said. "Now, why don't you hit the bathroom and get some of the dust off, and we'll get ready for supper. I could smell the barbecue when we pulled up."

I had just finished braiding Taylor's hair when there was a knock at the bedroom door. I went, expecting Angus, shocked into courtesy by the splendour of his surroundings. But when I opened the door it wasn't my son who was standing there, it was Christy Sinclair.

She didn't wait to be asked in. She walked past me and sat down on the bed. She was still wearing the overalls and striped shirt she'd had on in the car, but she'd splashed water on her face, and her hair curled damply at the temples. Christy never wore makeup. Her good looks were the kind that didn't need help, and that afternoon, as she smoothed her hair nervously and tried a tentative smile, I was puzzled again at her mystery.

Anyone who walked into that room would have been struck by the sum of Christy Sinclair's blessings. Physically, she had great charm; moreover, she was bright and educated and privileged. But somewhere, buried in her psyche, was a dark kink that distorted her perceptions and subverted her life.

I went over and sat beside her on the bed. My presence seemed to encourage her. She moved closer.

"I'm sorry about that business in the car, Jo," she said. "I know that kind of language is totally unacceptable to you."

I was horrified. "Christy, this isn't a problem of diction. It wasn't your language that upset me. It was the way you dismissed Bernice Morin. Whatever Bernice's life was like, her death was a terrible thing."

What I said seemed a statement of the obvious, but my words hit Christy like a blow. The smile faded, and when she spoke her voice trembled.

"Understand one thing, Joanne. Your death would be a terrible thing. Mieka's death would be a terrible thing. But when girls like Bernice die, it's just biological destiny. They're born with a gene that makes them self-destruct. They're all the same – antisocial, impulsive. They take risks that people like you and Mieka wouldn't. They never learn. They just keep taking risks, and sooner or later their luck runs out."

I felt cold. "Luck had nothing to do with it, Christy. Bernice Morin was murdered. She didn't self-destruct."

Christy's voice was weary. "It was her fault, Jo. Believe me, I know. I've done a lot of reading on genetic profiles. These girls are born with a gene for self-destruction. Nobody can change what's going to happen to them. Whatever girls like Bernice do, the disease is in them. It's just a matter of time."

"I refuse to believe that," I said.

"That doesn't make it any less true," she said quietly. Then she did a surprising thing. She reached down and pulled off the wide silver band she always wore around her wrist and held it out to me.

"You always said you admired this, Jo. I'd like you to have it."

I didn't want the bracelet. At that moment, I didn't want anything that would connect me to Christy Sinclair. But as I looked at the smooth circle of silver on the palm of her hand, I didn't know how to refuse. I took it. When I slipped it on my wrist, it was still warm from her body.

The bracelet was engraved with Celtic lettering, and I read the words aloud: "Wandering Soul Pray For Me."

Christy smiled. "I will," she said. She touched the silver band with her forefinger. "I love this bracelet, Jo, but I love you more. I didn't want you to go on thinking I was a bad person."

I moved closer to her. "Oh, Christy, I never thought you were bad. I've never felt as if I knew you at all. If you could just –"

I never finished the sentence. There was a knock at the door. Taylor came running out of the bathroom to answer it, and the moment was lost. Christy stood up and moved toward the doorway; she looked at the man who was standing there, then turned to me.

"Thank you for taking the bracelet, Jo. People aren't always what they seem, you know."

I went over to say goodbye, but she was gone.

"That's the worst introduction I've ever had," said the man in the doorway, "so I'll try to make up for it." He was holding a drink and he offered it to me. "Vodka and tonic with a twist. Your daughter said that's what you like on a hot day."

I took a long swallow from the drink. "God bless Mieka," I said. "It's turning into a vodka kind of afternoon."

He laughed. "I'm having one of those afternoons myself. I'll keep you company. Incidentally, I'm Greg's uncle, Keith Harris."

"I've seen you on television a thousand times," I said. "You're much nicer looking in person."

"So are you," he said. "But I have a more politically correct compliment for you. I read a review copy of your book on Andy Boychuk. It's the most intelligent biography I've read in ten years. You're going to be on the best-seller list."

"Kind words and a cold drink. Keith, I really am glad to meet you at last. And the kids were so worried we wouldn't get along."

Keith raised his eyebrows. "I tried to reassure Greg," he said, "but I think he and Mieka were convinced that the moment you and I met, we'd lock horns."

The talk of locked horns caught Taylor's attention. She was too young for metaphor. She moved between us and looked up expectantly.

"This is my daughter Taylor," I said. "Taylor, this is Mr. Harris. He's Greg's uncle."

Keith dropped to his knees to be eye level with Taylor. I saw her look with interest at his tanned and balding head. So did Keith.

"No horns," he said. "Although your mother might have been surprised to discover that, too. When people talk about locking horns with somebody they just mean they don't get along very well."

"Why wouldn't you and Jo get along?" Taylor asked.

"Because our politics are different," he said. "I work for one party, and your mother works for another party. Not much of a reason to fight, when you come right down to it."

But Taylor was not interested in politics. "We saw a field of swans," she said. "When we were in the car, we saw a field of swans. They were resting on their way home to the Arctic Circle. That's north," she added helpfully.

"Sounds better than my afternoon," he said. "I spent the last hour on the phone talking to . . . Well, never mind who I was talking to. It's boring. I can't offer you any swans, but if you and your mother come outside, I can show you the hill where once a long time ago a man saw a million buffalo coming down to the water."

Taylor looked up at him, dark eyes keen with interest. "A million buffalo," she said. "I wish I'd seen that."

He smiled at her. "I wish I had, too," he said, and with the easy camaraderie of people who've known each other for years, the three of us started toward the lake.

Angus caught up with us when we were halfway down the hill. He was running and his face shone with sweat and excitement. "There are frogs down there. Little ones –"

"No," I said.

"No to what?"

"No, you can't ask Mieka for a jar. No, you can't capture them and sell them. No, you can't take any back to the city and give them to your friends."

"I'm not a kid, Mum," he said. "Come on, Taylor. Let's go down to the lake and look at frogs. But don't get your hopes up. We already heard the answer about taking one home. See you, Mr. Harris," he said.

We watched them run toward the lake. "You've met my son?" I asked.

Keith nodded. "When I was getting ice, Angus was in the kitchen looking for . . ." He trailed off innocently.

"For a jar," I said.

"I've been in politics all my life, Joanne. I'm not walking into that one. Now, come on, and I'll show you where Peter Hourie saw that amazing sight. If you'd like, that is."

"I'd like," I said.

We walked down to the shore and looked up at the hill. "It was right over there," he said. "Hourie had just started building up Fort Qu'Appelle, and he was camped out here with some of his men. They looked over there and the buffalo were coming down to the water. Hourie and his group stayed here twenty-four hours, and the buffalo never stopped coming. They really did estimate there were a million animals in that herd. It must have sounded like the end of the world."

For the next half-hour we sat on the grass, talking about everything and nothing: the buffalo hunts, politics, friendships. Taylor and Angus, absorbed in the mysteries of the shore, were wading contentedly in the water that lapped the stony beach. The smell of barbecue and the sounds of music drifted down from the house. Finally, sun-warmed and at peace, I lay on the grass and closed my eyes.

"Happy?" Keith asked.

"God's in Her Heaven. All's right with the world," I murmured.

I'd almost drifted off to sleep when I heard Mieka's voice. "Here we were, worried sick that you two were going to kill each other and all you've done is put one another to sleep."

I sat up, rubbed my eyes and looked at Keith.

He shrugged. "Vodka and sunshine. A lethal combination."

Mieka shook her head. "Time to straighten up, Keith. Your dad's car just pulled in. Lorraine says he'll want to see you as soon as he gets settled."

"I'll be right up," Keith said, and he sounded weary and sad.

"Troubles?" I asked.

"My father," Keith said. "Blaine had a cerebral hemorrhage at Easter. It's hard to be with him now. For seventy-five years he was one man, and now he's another. The worst thing is he knows. He knows everything."

Keith stood up and held his hand out to me. "Do you want to come up to the house and meet Blaine? He's always enjoyed the company of intelligent women."

"I'd be honoured," I said. Then we called the kids and walked up the hill.

Keith's father was sitting in a wheelchair by the pool. Even the ravages of his illness hadn't eroded Blaine Harris's dignity. He was wearing golf clothes, expensive and well-cut, and he was beautifully groomed. But there were surprising notes: his white hair was so long it had been combed into a ponytail, and he was wearing not golf shoes but moccasins, soft and intricately beaded. He looked like a man on the verge of embracing another lifestyle.

When he saw his son, Blaine Harris raised his left hand in greeting, and garbled sounds escaped his throat. Keith went to him and kissed the top of his head.

His tone with his father was warm and matter of fact. "Blaine, this is Mieka's mother, Joanne. She teaches political science at the university and she's written a pretty fair book about Andy Boychuk."

Blaine made muffled noises that even I recognized as disapproval.

Keith looked at me. "My father's politics are somewhat to the right of mine." He turned back to his father. "Blaine, it's a wonderful book. We can start reading it tonight if you like."

Blaine made a swooping gesture toward me with his good arm. "Pancakes," he said.

Beside me, Taylor, recognizing another practitioner of the non sequitur, laughed appreciatively.

Keith patted his father's hand. "Yes, Dad, Joanne's book deals with campaigns, mostly the provincial ones."

The old man made a growling sound in the back of his throat.

Keith shook his head. "Yeah, Dad, I know it's awful when all the words are in there and they just won't come out. But what the hell, eh? You've got me. Now come on, it's time to eat."

It was a fine spring meal: barbecued lamb, the first tender shoots of asparagus, carrots, new potatoes, strawberry shortcake.

We sat outside at the tables around the pool I'd noticed earlier. I was surprised to see that Mieka had asked Christy to sit with Greg and her. Christy had changed clothes; she was wearing a white dress that looked cool and elegant. When Lorraine Harris joined them, I noticed she was wearing white, too. Midway through the meal, Greg and Mieka left to greet some latecomers, and as Lorraine and Christy bent toward one another, deep in conversation, I thought they looked like a scene from *The Great Gatsby*: handsome women in dazzling white, insulated by their money against the sordid and the wretched.

The kids and I sat with Keith and his father. Eating was a torturous process for Blaine Harris. He had the use of his left arm, but as he lifted his fork from his plate to his mouth, the signals sometimes got scrambled. His hand would stop, and Blaine would look at the fork hanging in midair as if it were an apparition. It was agony to watch, but Keith eased the situation. He was quick and unobtrusive when his father needed help, but he didn't hover, and he kept the conversation light.

To celebrate Greg's and Mieka's engagement, there were going to be fireworks later. Keith told the kids that when he'd been in Macau for the Chinese New Year in February, the fireworks had been loud enough to blow his eardrums out. He said the streets had been filled with people from Hong Kong because firecrackers were illegal there.

"And they're not illegal in Macau?" Angus asked approvingly.

"Nothing's illegal in Macau," he said. "The restaurants serve endangered species in the soup."

Angus shuddered.

"To build up your blood for the cold winter months," Keith said.

"Jo makes us take vitamin C," Taylor said.

"Probably a more responsible move environmentally," Keith said.

When Keith took his father into the house to rest before the fireworks, Angus turned to me. "Mr. Harris is a really neat guy, you know."

"Meaning?"

Angus grinned. "Meaning, I think it's about time you had a man in your life."

"Thanks, Angus, I'll take that under advisement."

"You wouldn't not go out with him because of politics, would you?"

"Nope," I said, "but it would be a problem. Keith is a good friend of the prime minister's, you know. In fact, a lot of people think Keith was the one who got him in as leader."

Angus grimaced. "Well, we all make mistakes."

"Yeah," I said, "but that one was a lulu."

Angus laughed. "I still think he's a nice guy."

I looked at the house. "There he is," I said, "bringing me coffee and brandy."

"Then we're out of here," said Angus. "Come on, T. Let's see if we can find a radio and catch the baseball game." He gave me the high sign. "Be nice to him, Mum."

I was. When I took my first sip of brandy, I leaned back in my chair. "What a perfect night," I said.

"'Calm was the even and clear was the sky, and the new-budding flowers did spring,'" Keith said.

"Dryden," I said, "'An Evening's Love.'"

Keith Harris looked at me in amazement. "There's not another woman in Canada who would have known that."

"No," I agreed, "there isn't. You're in luck. It's a magic night."

"You wouldn't have a spell that would keep Lorraine away, would you?" Keith said. "She's about to swoop. We're going to be organized for some after-dinner fun, I can tell by the glint in her eyes."

Then in a cloud of Chanel, Lorraine Harris was upon us. She embraced her brother-in-law, then she turned and bent to kiss the air by my cheek. Out of nowhere, a poem from childhood floated to the top of my consciousness:

> I do not like you, Dr. Fell.
> The reason why I cannot tell.
> But this I know and I know well.
> I do not like you, Dr. Fell.

I do not like you, Lorraine Harris, I thought. But what I said was, "You look wonderful, Lorraine. That's a beautiful suit."

"Sharkskin," she said. She sat down on the arm of Keith's chair and balanced her clipboard on her knee. She was tanned, and the setting sun warmed her skin to the colour of dark honey and made her grey eyes startling. She was a stunning woman, and her most striking feature was her hair. In defiance of all the rules about how women should wear their hair after forty, Lorraine's grey hair was almost waist length. That night she had clasped it at the back with a silver barrette, and as she talked, she reached back and pulled the length of her hair over her shoulder. The effect was riveting.

"How do you two feel about croquet?" she asked.

I smiled at her. "I haven't played croquet in thirty-five years, but I think it's a terrific idea."

Keith sighed. "If Jo's in, I'm in."

Lorraine's grey eyes narrowed. "So you two are getting along, after all," she said. "There'll be some raised eyebrows about that."

"Not any eyebrows that matter," Keith said mildly.

Lorraine looked at him quickly, then she pulled part of a deck of cards out of her jacket pocket and held it out to me. "Choose one, Joanne."

I pulled out a jack of diamonds.

"All you have to do is find the other people who have jacks," she said, "that'll be your team."

Keith reached over and took the cards from her. He sorted through it and pulled out a jack of clubs. "That's me on your team, Jo." Then he found the other two jacks. "That's one for Angus and one for Taylor. Get the word out, Lorraine. The Jacks are the team to beat."

A flicker of annoyance crossed her face. "It's supposed to be random," she said as she wrote our names down on her list, "an icebreaker. But obviously you two have already broken the ice."

She finished writing and stood. "Come up to the tent in about twenty minutes and see who you're supposed to play." Then her face softened, and she smiled at someone behind me. "You have to be Peter," she said. "I made Mieka show me your picture when Greg said you were going to be a groomsman."

I turned and there was my oldest son. For a split second he looked unfamiliar. He seemed taller, his face was sun-burned, and he had a new and terrible haircut. I thought he looked sensational.

I jumped up and threw my arms around him. "I'm not going to let you go back to Swift Current," I said. "I've decided I don't believe in kids having independent lives."

Angus was sitting on the ground trying to get an old portable radio to work. "I think Pete probably figured that one out the night you called him three times because you thought he sounded weird."

Peter looked at his brother. "Actually, Mum was right." He turned to me. "I wasn't going to say anything until you could see that I was still alive, but that time you called a cow had just kicked me in the head."

I shot Angus a look of triumph. "Okay, okay," he said, scraping at the batteries of the radio with his Swiss Army knife. "You win. You're psychotic, Mum."

"Thank you," I said, "and the word is psychic."

Peter introduced himself to Lorraine and Keith, then Taylor asked to hear the story of the cow. It was a good story, and Pete told it well. We were all still laughing when Christy came down from the house. She touched Pete on the shoulder, and as he turned I saw the light go out of his face.

Christy saw it, too, and despite our history I felt a rush of sympathy for her. In the months they were together, I don't think Christy ever really understood what she wanted from Peter. But that night at the lake she knew. She wanted him to be in love with her, and when she saw his face, she knew he wasn't. It was a bad moment, and I was glad when Peter took her hands in his.

"You look beautiful, Christy," he said. "You really do. That dress is a knockout."

In fact, it was a simple dress, white, scoop-necked and short-sleeved. A dress for a summer party. And she was wearing shoes for a summer party, white Capezio flats of the softest leather. Taylor couldn't take her eyes off them. Finally, she knelt on the grass and touched one. "Dancing shoes," she said.

Peter slid his arm around Christy's shoulder. "Would you like to dance? I don't know what they've got planned here tonight, but I can hear music somewhere."

"I'd love to dance," she said, and there was such longing in her voice that I turned away, embarrassed.

It was almost eight-thirty. The sun had moved low in the sky, and a swath of golden light swept from the west lawn to the lake. As Peter and Christy walked to the house, they followed that path of light. They looked like the happily-ever-after picture at the end of a fairy tale.

On the ground beside me, Angus gave the portable radio one last adjustment with his knife. Suddenly the radio blared to life, and a man's voice, disjointed and unnaturally loud, cut through the night. "... that was found by children in a stairwell two blocks from the murder site may be the weapon used in the stabbing death of seventeen-year-old Bernice Morin. Tonight, the provincial lab is analyzing blood found on the scalpel to see if it matches the blood type of the victim. As well, pathologists are attempting to correlate a number of small nicks in the cutting edge of the surgical scalpel with the wounds inflicted on ..." The radio fell silent.

As soon as she heard the words, Christy broke away from Peter and turned to face us. For a terrible moment, she stood frozen, staring at the radio, her eyes wide with horror. Then she turned and ran toward the house. Peter went after her. He got to the veranda just as she slammed the door. He hesitated, then he opened the door and disappeared into the darkness of the house.

Lorraine Harris sat looking thoughtfully at the spot on the lawn where Christy had acted out her curious tableau. Then she shook herself out of her reverie and checked her watch.

"Time to get the croquet started before we lose the light," she said. "I'll put Peter and his fiancé on the same team."

"His friend," I said, "they're not engaged."

"Well, his friend told me they were engaged," Lorraine said. She wrote the names on her list. "Keith, you might as well bring your crew along now. It's getting late. People can pick their own teams."

She stood, and we followed her as she strode up the hill and into the house. I started to go inside, too, then I stopped. "Remember the wrestling," I said under my breath, "let them be. They're not children. They'll work it out."

A striped tent had been set up on the west lawn. It was filled with people and laughter. There was a well-stocked bar set up on one side; beside it, on a small table, an orchard of fruit floated in a crystal bowl of punch. In the centre of the tent, Lorraine Harris stood with her clipboard arranging teams, setting up games. There was a master list on a flip chart beside her. I checked the list.

"We're playing the Deuces," I said to Keith.

The Deuces turned out to be the rest of Greg's grooms-men, four young men with the flawless good looks that come with a lifetime of solid nutrition and expensive ortho-donture. The game wasn't as one-sided as I'd feared. When it was over, we hadn't distinguished ourselves, but the Deuces hadn't blown our doors out, and as we walked to the tent we were happy. Inside, the noise level had risen, and the level in the liquor bottles had fallen.

From the talk in the tent it was apparent that croquet had caught on. There were challenges and counter-challenges. On the flip chart someone had written the names of the winners of the first games and the matches for the second set.

Keith checked the chart. "Losers' tournament starts at seven-thirty tomorrow morning," he said.

I snapped open two bottles of Heineken and handed one to Keith. "I've already forgotten what you just said. Now, come on, let's find the kids and get ready for the fireworks."

"Jo, I promised my dad I'd sit up on the veranda with him and watch. Do you mind?"

"Of course not," I said. "I'm going to see if Peter and Christy will come down and watch with us from the dock. I can't figure out what's going on there, but whatever it is, she and Peter might find it easier to be away from strangers."

Keith and I walked to the house together. Blaine Harris was already on the veranda waiting. The woman who had served our dinner was with him, tucking a blanket around his legs, but when Blaine saw his son, he shook the woman off.

Keith called to his father, then he turned to me. "I'll find you after the fireworks. I'll bring that bottle of brandy, take the chill off our bones."

"I'll be waiting," I said.

Keith bent and kissed my cheek, and from the veranda, the old man growled in disapproval.

"His bark is worse than his bite," Keith said mildly. Then he kissed me again.

When I knocked on Peter's door, he opened it so quickly I thought he must have been on his way out.

"How are you doing?" I asked.

"I'm okay," he said.

"And Christy?"

"She's out on the lake," he said. "Canoeing. She said even when she was a kid, she did that when she was upset. It calmed her down."

"Where did she find a place to canoe in Estevan?" I said. "That's pretty arid country down there."

Peter shrugged, "You know Christy. Anyway, if you want, you can ask her when she gets back. She says she has to talk to you. It's urgent."

I stepped close to him. "What's going on, Peter?"

He gave me an awkward pat on the shoulder. "I don't know, Mum. I thought I did, but now I'm not sure."

"Whatever it is, Peter, I'm on your side.".

"I know," he said softly. He looked very young and very troubled. In that moment, I knew that, this time, having me on his side wasn't going to be enough.

The kids and I walked to the dock alone. Just as we arrived, Mieka came and dragged her brother off to the beach, where Greg and his friends had lit a bonfire and set up the drinks.

"You look like you could use some company that isn't Angus," she said. "Mum, you and the kids are welcome, too, but Greg swears the dock is the place to be because you get the best view of the lake. That's where he always sat when he was little." She shook her head. "I can't believe Lorraine got everybody to set off their fireworks for our party instead of waiting till Monday night."

"She's a very persuasive woman," I said. "But I'm with her on this. I think your engagement's more important than a dead Queen's birthday."

Taylor grabbed my hand and gave it a yank. "Jo, come on. Don't talk any more, let's go."

We agreed to sit at the end of the dock. I'd brought blankets, and as Taylor curled up against me, I pulled a blanket around her and we looked at the lake. There were boats out there, lazily circling, waiting for the fireworks. I thought I could pick out Christy in her white party dress, but the canoe was so far away I couldn't be sure. The fishy-bait smell of the lake brought memories of other lakes, other summers, and I let my mind float. I could feel Taylor getting heavier in my arms.

"You're falling asleep, T.," Angus said.

She started. "No, I'm not."

"Just resting her eyes, Angus," I said. "Remember, that's what you used to say."

"Right, Mum," he said. "Want me to tell you one of the stories I heard at scout camp last year, T.?"

"Oh, yeah," she said.

"Not too scary," I said. "I want to sleep tonight."

So Angus told all the old stories: the babysitter and the anonymous calls, the kids parked in lovers' lane when the ghost of her first boyfriend comes and bangs on the roof of the car. And Taylor and I screamed and giggled and then somewhere around the lake a cottager put his tuba to his lips and played "God Save the Queen," and the fireworks began.

Greg had told us the Victoria Day ritual was as old as the

cottages. The anthem, then one by one, the cottages set off
their fireworks from the beach until the lake had been
ringed with rockets.

This year it was the Harris's turn to begin. Greg had set
up a rocket in the sand. As he knelt to light it, I could hear
Mieka's voice, "Be careful. Be careful. Get back." And I
thought she was her mother's daughter after all.

There was a small flash of light, and then the rocket went
screaming up into the dark night; it hung there in space for
a heartbeat, then it shattered into a shower of brilliant
sparks, gold, green, pink.

"Coloured stars," Taylor said, and her eyes were wide
with wonder. They kept getting wider. The Harrises were
presenting an impressive array of fireworks. When the last
stars from the last rocket fell to the ground, Greg came over
to the dock with a packet of sparklers. As the moonlight hit
his face, I looked for traces of Keith's side of the family in
him, but I couldn't see any.

Greg Harris had his mother's colouring and her grey eyes
but, curiously, not her good looks. The week before, he'd
called the tux rental place from our house, and I'd heard him
say, "I'm just an ordinary-looking guy, so nothing too Ralph
Lauren." He was right. He was ordinary looking. He was also
kind and bright and funny, and crazy about Mieka. Every
time I looked at him, I counted my blessings.

As he handed the sparklers to Angus and went through
the warnings, I counted my blessings again.

"Best part coming up, Angus. You're in charge. Watch
your eyes, and don't light Taylor on fire." Greg grinned at
me. "How'd I do, Jo? Cover all the bases."

I smiled at him. "You always do," I said.

We stood and watched as Angus, newly mature, lit the
sparklers carefully and handed them to Taylor. She had
never seen a sparkler, and her face was solemn as she wrote

her name in letters that glowed and vanished in the dark summer night. And then there was a whooshing sound and the fireworks from the next cottage began, sputtering, climbing to the stars and exploding.

"I'd better get back to the party," Greg said. "From the sound of things they need a moral centre over there." He gave me a quick hug. "Have fun, Jo. If you need anything, holler."

For an hour the rockets soared and coloured lights rained down on the lake. When I saw a man jump from the dock next to ours onto the beach, I said to the kids, "Last one. Greg says the last family always has to buy the most expensive stuff for the grand finale."

Taylor, already punchy from excitement and tiredness, leaned forward expectantly. But nothing happened. Then I heard a man's voice, very faint.

"Help," he said. "Someone help me. There's been an accident."

I looked toward the beach. Peter and Mieka were standing by the bonfire, their faces ruddy from the heat and reflected flames. They hadn't heard a thing. People had started dancing, and the music must have drowned out the man's voice.

"Take your sister up to the house and get some help," I said to Angus. Then I ran along the dock, jumped onto the rocky shore and moved toward the voice in the darkness.

The man was still holding the rocket that was going to be the grand finale, but it didn't look as if he'd be setting it off that night. He seemed to be on the verge of shock.

"She's drowned. I just got here from the city. I got tied up at the office." He pointed to the pilings under the dock. "There's a girl down there. I think she's dead."

"Call an ambulance," I said. "I'll do CPR until someone comes. Go on," I said.

I went over to the pilings and pulled the woman's body to the beach. Then I knelt on the rocks, leaned forward and tried to breathe life into the limp body of Christy Sinclair. I'd completed four cycles of compressions and ventilations when one of Greg's friends came and relieved me. I'd talked to him earlier in the tent. He'd said he was an intern, and this was his first night away from the hospital in two weeks. We spelled each other off for what seemed like hours. Finally, he rocked back on his heels and said, "We lost her."

For the first time, I looked up. The guests from the engagement party were huddled in silent knots along the length of the dock. Greg and Peter were directly above me. Mieka was behind her brother, with her arms locked around his waist as if she was holding him back. But Peter didn't look as if he was going anywhere. He seemed frozen, and his face as he looked at Christy showed disbelief. I moved toward Christy. One of her Capezios had fallen off. She had always been immaculate, and it didn't seem right to let people see her with one foot bare and her white party dress sodden and weedy. I leaned forward and took off the other shoe and laid it beside her body. Then I wiped a flume of weeds from the skirt of her dress. She was so still. The animation that had always illuminated her face was gone. The stillness changed her, made her look as if, already, she had become the citizen of a far-off land. But her mouth hadn't changed; it had curved into its familiar sardonic line. Christy Sinclair was greeting death with her sidelong pickerel smile.

CHAPTER

4

The RCMP officer who was first on the scene after we discovered Christy Sinclair's body was a round-faced constable named Kequahtooway. He wasn't much older than the young men and women at the party, but he took charge easily. The first thing he did was call headquarters for reinforcements. It was a prudent move. There were sixty-three people at that party, and one of them was dead. The second thing Constable Kequahtooway did was try to bring some order to the chaos.

Less than an hour earlier, Mieka's and Greg's friends, handsome in their summer pastels, had been careless and confident. Nothing would ever hurt them. Christy's death had made them all vulnerable. Now, dazed and disoriented, they turned for reassurance to a young Indian man wearing the uniform of the RCMP and the traditional braids of his people. It was a scene that would have surprised everybody's grandparents.

Constable Kequahtooway blocked off the area where Christy had been found, then he set up a place for questioning in the tent. It had been half an hour since I'd sent Angus up to the house with Taylor; suddenly, I needed to know that they were safe. As soon as I turned down the hall on the main floor of the house, I ran into Keith Harris.

"My God, what's happening?" he said. "We were watching the fireworks. Everything seemed fine, and then the police car pulled up. As soon as he saw it, my father just went crazy." As if on cue, a howling noise came from Blaine Harris's room at the end of the hall. Keith winced. "He's been like this ever since the police came. Jo, what's going on?"

"Peter's friend Christy was in some sort of accident down on the beach. Nobody knows what happened, but, Keith . . . Christy didn't make it. She's dead." It was the first time I had said the words, and I shuddered at their finality. "I still can't believe it," I said.

Keith reached out and touched my cheek. "I'm so sorry," he said. He looked toward his father's room. "I've got to find a doctor for Blaine. He can't go on like this. I'll be right back. As soon as I get my dad taken care of, I'll find you, and we can talk."

"I'd like that," I said.

Keith took me in his arms. It was the briefest of embraces, but that night it was good to be close to another human being, good to have an ally against the things that go bump in the night.

The room Taylor and I were sharing was next door to Lorraine's room, or what was normally Lorraine's room. She'd put Blaine Harris in there because it was on the main floor. As I walked down the hall toward the room, I could hear the sounds he was making. He sounded furious. There was an edge of frustration in his cries, and I thought of the inchoate fury of my kids when they were very young and didn't have the words to tell me what they wanted. Just as I opened the door to our room, the old man managed to form a word.

"Killdeer," he said, and as he pronounced the word, his voice was as loud and as penetrating as the bird's call.

Taylor was sleeping, and Angus was sitting in a chair by the window.

"Scrunch over and make room for me," I said.

I squeezed in beside him and pulled him close. "How are you doing?" I asked.

"Okay, I guess. Greg came by and told me that it was Christy down there. He said he'd stay with me, but I told him Mieka probably needed him more than I did."

He looked up at me. "I didn't like Christy, Mum. She was always pulling stuff with Pete, and what she said in the car about getting married gave me the creeps."

"Me, too," I said.

"All the same . . ." His voice cracked, and he started again. "All the same, now that she's dead, I feel like a real butt head."

For a moment we sat in silence, absorbed in our thoughts. Finally, I leaned toward my youngest son. "I fed like a butt head, too. Listen, Angus, I haven't got many answers about this, but I do know it's normal to feel rotten when someone dies and we haven't treated her as well as we should have. You and I are going to feel bad about Christy for a long time. There's no way around that. But there's one thing we have to hang on to here. It wasn't our fault that Christy died. It was an accident.

"Now, come on, it's late. You should try to get some sleep. I'll walk you to your room, or would you rather stay here?"

"I'd better go to my own room," he said. "Pete's in there with me, you know. He might want to talk."

He looked at me, and we both smiled. Pete had never been much of a talker.

"He'll be glad you're there, anyway," I said.

I checked Taylor. She was sleeping deeply.

"Come on," I said. "Let's get you settled. At least over there, you won't have to listen to Greg's poor grandfather."

"What's the matter with him, Mum?"

"I think he's frustrated," I said. "I think he's mad because he has something important on his mind, and he can't talk any more."

After I got Angus settled, I went outside. It seemed as if there were as many police as there were guests. There were uniforms everywhere. I walked to the tent and looked in. Peter was there, sitting across the table from a young woman in an RCMP uniform. I went and sat at one of the wrought-iron tables that had been set out around the pool for dinner. If I couldn't help my son, I could at least be somewhere he could see me.

I was sitting there feeling powerless and sad when Greg came and sat across from me. The lights from the tent leached the colour from his cheeks and knifed lines in the planes of his face. He looked twenty years older than he had when he'd come to the dock to bring the kids their sparklers.

"Thanks for checking on Angus," I said.

He shrugged. "I wanted to do something." He looked at me. "You know what I've been thinking about?"

"Woody Allen," I said.

He smiled. Greg's passion for Woody Allen was a family joke. When his relationship with Mieka started to get serious, Greg had come over one snowy Friday night with an armload of videos. "I think it's time you met God," he had said as he loaded *Annie Hall* into our VCR.

That weekend we had a Woody Allen festival, and Greg, smart enough to know he sounded like a groupie in a Woody movie, explained every frame of every movie. After that, Woody had become a part of all our lives. We teased Greg about him, but it had been terrific for all of us to have a touchstone to share with the man Mieka loved.

That terrible night at the lake Woody seemed to work his magic once again. At the mention of his name, Greg seemed to relax. "For once you're wrong, Jo. I wasn't thinking of Woody, but now that you mention him . . . Do you know what he said about death? 'I'm not afraid of death. I just don't want to be there when it happens.'"

"Woody and the rest of the thinking population," I said.

"Right." Greg picked up a matchbook someone had left behind, took out a match and lit it. He watched it flame, then burn out. His young face was stricken. "What I was thinking about was Christy. Jo, they found the boat she was in – it was almost in the middle of the lake. It was the red canoe my mother gave me for my sixteenth birthday. There was a half-empty bottle of rye in it. And, Jo, there was an empty pill bottle in the boat, too. My mother sometimes takes these tranquilizers, and Christy must have found the bottle in Mum's bathroom cupboard. Anyway, it was empty. The police aren't saying anything, of course, but from the questions they were asking me, I think they're treating this as a suicide."

I thought of Christy's face in the moments after Peter came, when she knew that whatever future they had together wouldn't include love.

"Oh, God, poor Christy," I said. Then I thought of my son. "Greg, does Peter know?"

He shook his head. "I don't think so. I had to go down and identify the boat and my mother's pills. I just overheard things. I'm sure the police aren't telling people yet." He pushed himself back from the table. "I'd better see how Mieka's doing. This has been a pretty awful night for her, too."

"She's lucky she has you," I said.

He smiled. "That goes both ways, you know."

After he left, I felt myself slump. When Constable Kequahtooway came over and slid into the chair Greg had been sitting in, it took an effort of will to look up. "P. Kequahtooway," his badge said. I had heard one of the other cops call him Perry.

Up close, Perry Kequahtooway looked very young, but he was assured and he was thorough. I didn't find his questions painful; I had already moved into that zone of blunted emotion that comes when I know the worst has happened. I was able to replay the scenes of the evening pretty much without emotion: the time Christy had arrived at our house; the drive down; when I had seen her; when I hadn't seen her. Constable Kequahtooway took it all down without comment. Then he looked at me and asked a question I wasn't prepared for. "Did you know that Christy Sinclair listed you as next of kin on the emergency card in her wallet?"

I was dumfounded. "That doesn't make sense," I said. "I'm just the mother of a boy she was going out with. She has family in Estevan. They sent her money regularly. I mean she said they did, and they must have. Christy's only income was what she earned as a teaching assistant – there's no way she could have afforded the life she lived on a graduate student's stipend." I realized I was talking more to myself than to him. When I looked up, he was waiting patiently.

"And the name of the people in Estevan is Sinclair?" he asked.

"I guess so," I said weakly. "At least that's what Christy said."

"But you didn't believe her?" Constable Kequahtooway asked.

"She was a complicated young woman," I said.

Constable Perry Kequahtooway looked at me patiently. "Tell me about it," he said.

"There's not much to tell," I said, "except that sometimes Christy had her own perception of reality."

"She told lies," he said softly.

I nodded. Behind him, I could see Peter coming out of the tent, alone.

"Can I go to see my son now?" I asked.

Constable Kequahtooway looked surprised. "Of course, Mrs. Kilbourn."

"Did you tell him that Christy committed suicide?" I asked.

Suddenly, he was tense. "What makes you think she did?"

"Greg Harris told me about the empty pill bottle in the bottom of the canoe."

"An empty pill bottle doesn't make a suicide, Mrs. Kilbourn. I'd appreciate it if you kept your theories to yourself. I really would. We don't want to muddy the waters here."

I caught up with Peter at the front door to the house.

"How about some coffee?" I said. "It's getting cold out there. Or tea?"

He shook his head. "Nothing, thanks. I think I'd like to walk, though."

He started toward the road, and I followed.

"The beach is pretty crowded, with the police and everybody," he said.

We stopped at a hairpin turn in the road and walked toward a jut of land that overlooked the lake. Beneath us we could see the police checking the beach. The red canoe had been pulled up on shore.

I touched his arm. "Peter, I know this is a bad time to ask, but the police say that Christy had a card in her wallet that listed me as her next of kin. Do you know anything about it?"

There was a full moon that night. In the pale light, my son seemed alien, not just older but metamorphosed, as if Christy's death had changed him into a different man.

"She was so fucked up," he said in a voice tight with pain. "She was so fucking fucked up."

Then he began to cry. I put my arms around him and held him as he sobbed out his grief. Finally, he wiped his eyes with the sleeve of his sweater. "We'd better get back," he said.

For a few minutes we walked in silence, then Peter stopped. "I wanted her out of my life, and now she is," he said. It sounded as if he was speaking more to himself than to me.

"Peter, can you talk about it? What happened with you two tonight?"

"I don't know, Mum. Everything seemed all right. All we were doing was going up to the house to dance, remember? It was all so quick. Christy said she'd talked to you about us getting married the same day Mieka and Greg did, and I said okay. Then that radio Angus was playing with came on, and Christy just bugged out. I went after her, but when I finally found out what room she was in, she wouldn't let me in. I know you'll find this hard to understand, but it didn't really worry me when Christy wouldn't talk to me."

"Why?"

He raked his hand through his hair. "She did it all the time. She never needed a reason. Once she told me it was a compulsion – that she had to keep testing me to see how far she could go before I'd stop loving her."

I ran my forefinger over the lettering on the bracelet Christy had given me. "Did she get to that point tonight?"

"She got past that point a long time ago," he said bleakly.

"Then what in the name of God were you doing back together?" I asked.

He put his head down and started walking faster.

"Peter, please, I know you don't want to talk about this, but we have to. This isn't *The Brady Bunch*. This is real. A young woman died tonight. If you didn't care about her, what was she doing here talking about marriage?"

Suddenly the answer was there, and I wondered if I'd been waiting for flaming letters in the sky.

"She was pregnant," I said.

He nodded. "We would have gotten married. That wasn't what upset her."

I felt as if I'd been kicked in the stomach. "What then? What made her decide to . . ."

"Decide to what, Mum?"

I could see the pulse beating in Peter's neck. He didn't need to hear speculations about Christy's death tonight. "Nothing, Pete. You look exhausted. What time did you get up this morning, anyway?"

"Five-thirty," he said. "Animals are early risers." For a beat he was silent, then he turned to me. "I wish I was back there now. I wish it was still this morning and none of this had happened."

I slid my arm around my son's waist, and together we started toward the house. We didn't say anything. There was nothing left to say.

When we got back, the house and grounds were still brilliantly lit. It would have been easy to believe there was still a celebration going on. But as I walked through the silent house I knew the party was over. Suddenly, I was so weary I had to force myself to turn the knob of the door to my room. Taylor had kicked off her bedclothes. I tucked her in, then I went over to my bed and collapsed. I didn't even turn down the bedspread.

That night was a troubled one for Blaine Harris, and that meant it was a troubled one for me. For hours, Keith's father seemed to drift in and out of anguish. Close to morning, I heard muffled voices on the other side of the wall, and the old man's voice was finally stilled. I couldn't sleep.

Every time I closed my eyes, Christy was there. The last time he saw her alive, Christy had told Peter she had to talk to me, that it was urgent. Why would she tell him that if she'd planned to take her own life? It didn't make sense.

When it was light enough to read the hands on my watch, I decided to give up. During the night Mieka had come in and crawled into bed with Taylor. As I walked to the bathroom, I stopped and looked at them. They were curled together spoon fashion, rosy, seeking out animal warmth in the time of trouble. It was instinct.

I showered and pulled on a fresh cotton dress and sandals. It was still cool, and I took a sweater out of my bag and walked to the kitchen to make coffee. In the half-light of dawn the kitchen was a ghostly place and shiningly perfect, although I knew the couple who worked for Lorraine Harris had made sandwiches and hot drinks for everyone late in the evening.

I found coffee in the cupboard, and as I waited for it to brew, I wandered into the sunroom next to the kitchen. Lorraine had set up an office in one corner of the room; a pretty rolltop desk faced the windows, and a small filing cabinet was tucked discreetly in the corner. There were two pictures on the desk. In one, Lorraine, elegant in black, her extravagant hair smoothed in a chignon, sat at a head table beaming up at a man giving a speech. I recognized some of the other people at the banquet. Like Lorraine, they were wheelers and dealers in the business community, people I knew because I had seen their pictures on the financial pages of the newspaper. The man who was speaking seemed familiar, but I couldn't place him. He must have been a major player in Lorraine's life, because he was in the second picture, too. This one was informal, a holiday picture, someplace where there were palm trees and white sand. In this photo, Lorraine and the man were wearing cruise clothes and they were both deeply tanned. The man was reaching out to touch a spray of flame-coloured hibiscus in Lorraine's hair. He looked smug and proprietorial, and I was glad it wasn't my hair he was touching.

I went to the kitchen, poured a mug of coffee and took it down to the dock. The sky was overcast, and mist was rising like smoke from the lake. I had the sense that I was the only person in the world. The morning had the cool menace of an Alex Colville painting. Across the lake was the hill where Peter Hourie and his men had seen the buffalo. A million buffalo. All dead now. Murdered into near extinction. Out of nowhere a phrase came into my mind – "too proud or too dumb to live" – and I thought of Bernice Morin sprawled over the garbage can outside Mieka's store and of Christy, her generous mouth frozen in a death grin. Two young women dead.

Through the grey mist I could see the yellow police tape marking off the beach where Christy had died. To the south, on the other side of the dock, more police tape marked off the beach where hours before young people had danced and laughed, privileged, enviable.

Suddenly I had the sense that I wasn't alone. I turned and behind me was Keith Harris. He was wearing a pale blue sport shirt. A shirt for a Saturday morning, except this wasn't going to be a day for golf and sun and gin and tonic in the clubhouse. His face was haggard.

"I looked for you last night," he said, "but I saw you were with your family. I didn't want to intrude. Did you get any sleep?"

"Not much," I said.

"Of course, your room's next to Blaine's. I'm sorry, Jo. That must have been the last thing you needed."

"He sounded so angry," I said. "My kids used to sound like that when they were little and they couldn't figure out how to get from point A to point B."

Keith sighed. "Most of the time I just deal with the situations that come up. Straightforward stuff, problem and solution. Then, every so often, like last night, I get a glimpse of what it must be like for him. That's when I go crazy."

"How long has he been like this?"

"Since Easter Sunday. I was with him when it happened. We were golfing. My dad had a putter in his hand, and suddenly he gave me this odd, preoccupied look and said, 'I don't know what to do with this.' I thought he was kidding and I made some joke. But he didn't laugh. He just stood there looking baffled.

"One of the other members of our foursome was a doctor. He knew right away. I went to the hospital with them, and I asked the neurologist to let me stay while they did the CAT scan. I don't think I've ever been so scared. There was this picture of my father's brain; on it, I could see a dark stain about the size of a robin's egg. That was the hemorrhage, and as I watched, the stain started spreading. And the neurologist said, very coolly: 'He just lost speech,' and then the stain elongated and spread, and he said, 'That was mobility. If it keeps augmenting there won't be much left.' And I looked at him, and I said, 'That's my father you're writing off, asshole,' and I walked out of the room."

Keith had been looking away from me, toward the lake. Suddenly he faced me. "Jo, I'm sorry. Sometimes, I think Blaine's becoming an obsession with me. I should be thinking about you. Do they know anything more about what happened last night?"

I shook my head. "I had a long talk with Constable Kequahtooway, but I think it's too early for them to know much for sure."

"Greg said he told you about the police finding that empty pill bottle in the canoe. You knew Christy Sinclair, Jo. Does that add up? Would she have committed suicide?"

"If you'd asked me yesterday, I would have said no. But now I'm not so sure. In the last twenty-four hours of her life, something went terribly wrong for Christy. I don't know what kinds of things she was dealing with. Except . . ." I stopped.

"Except what?" Keith said gently.

Suddenly, I was tired of secrets. I wanted somebody else to share the burden. "Christy was pregnant, Keith."

He looked stricken. "Poor Peter," he said, "to lose a child." It was such an odd thing to say, but somehow it was exactly right. I was feeling that loss, too.

When the wind came up, we walked to the house hand in hand. Keith brought coffee out, and we sat at one of the tables near the pool and talked about life and loss.

When Taylor came running out of the house, the mood shifted from the elegiac. She had chosen her own clothes from the suitcase; they were mismatched, and her blonde hair was tangled from sleep, but she was hotly eager to get the day underway. No one had told her about Christy.

She jumped on my lap and put her arms around me.

"And good morning to you, too," I said. "This is a great way to begin the day."

She looked around. "Can I go and get Angus?" she said.

"Let him sleep for a while, T.," I said. "He was up pretty late. Why don't you draw him a picture?"

Keith handed her a pen. "Sorry, I don't have paper," he said.

"I know where there's some," I said. I went into the tent. Lorraine's clipboard was still on the card table. I ripped a sheet from the pad where she'd written the names of the teams for croquet. I brought the paper out and handed it to Taylor.

"There's writing on it," Taylor said.

"Use the other side," I said. "Angus will be proud of how you're conserving trees."

She sat and drew, and Keith and I watched her.

When I'd finished my coffee, I stood up. "I'd better go see what's happening here. If there's anything I can do, I'll stay, but if not, I'm going back to the city. I'm sure Lorraine would be relieved to have everyone out right about now."

He smiled. "I think I'd better stick around till tomorrow. Blaine shouldn't be moved when he's like this. Besides, Lorraine has a touching belief that men are useful in a crisis. I'll call you as soon as I get back in the city."

I gave him my number, then I tapped Taylor on the shoulder.

"Come on, T. It's time to boogie."

Taylor handed me her drawing. "Here, for Angus," she said. It was a page full of frogs. "Since he can't take any real ones home with him," she explained.

"Great," I said. I looked at it again. "It really is great, Taylor." I showed it to Keith, and we walked to the house. When I got to my room, I slipped the picture into my bag and forgot about it.

The couple who worked for Lorraine Harris were busy in the kitchen making breakfast. I could smell the good aromas of bacon and toast and waffles. Some of the young people from the party were already eating. They were over the first shock, but as I looked at them, I knew it would be a long time before they recovered. Their voices, so exuberant the night before, were muted; even their gestures seemed careful and controlled, as if they were afraid of drawing attention to themselves.

Keith and I filled plates for ourselves and for Taylor. After we'd eaten, I poured a glass of juice and went up to check on Peter. I knocked at his door.

"It's okay. Come on in," he said.

He'd showered and dressed, but he looked terrible.

I handed him the juice. "They have breakfast downstairs," I said. "Can I bring you something?"

He took a tentative sip. "Thanks, Mum. I think I'll be doing pretty well if I manage to get this down."

"Pete, I think as soon as you're up to it, we should go back to the city. This place is a nightmare for everybody right now. If we went home, you could sit out in the sunshine with the dogs and be by yourself for a while."

Peter went to the corner, picked up the clothes he'd been wearing the night before and shoved them in his knapsack. "I'm ready when you are," he said.

After everyone had eaten, it didn't take us long to get organized. Mieka decided to stay at the lake with the Harrises. She said they needed her, and she was right. The doctor who came to check on Blaine had been alarmed about the deterioration in his condition. Greg wanted to stay with his grandfather, and Mieka wanted to be with Greg.

Peter said he'd feel better if he drove, and Angus volunteered to go with him. So just Taylor and I were riding in the Volvo for the trip back. As I started up the driveway, a yellow Buick hurtled out of the garage behind the house and turned onto the driveway. I had to brake to keep from hitting it. I don't think Lorraine Harris even saw me, but I saw her. She was wearing her horn-rimmed glasses, and her grey hair was loose. She disappeared over the hill in a split second, but as I drove carefully around one of the hairpin turns on the reserve road, I saw the buttercup-yellow Buick on the other side of the valley. Lorraine was really tearing up the highway. I thought she must be desperate to put miles between herself and the disaster she left behind.

It was the Saturday morning of a holiday weekend, and traffic on the highway into the city was light. When we passed Edenwold, I saw that the tundra swans had gone. Moved on north. I thought of Christy standing by the fence in the brilliant May sunshine: "If they're smart and lucky, they'll make it." Maybe, I thought. Maybe.

We were in Regina by ten-fifteen. As we drove through the city streets, we could see people in their front yards putting in bedding plants, visiting. The months of grey isolation were over; it was time to get reacquainted with the neighbours.

"How would you like to do that today?" I said to Taylor, pointing to a girl helping her mother garden.

She frowned. "I thought maybe we could get my new bike today, since we came back early. Maybe Angus could teach me how to ride it."

I hadn't told her about Christy yet, and I was dreading it. Taylor had already seen too much death in her young life. I remembered Angus's guilt and confusion about Christy the night before. Giving his sister bike-riding lessons might be just the distraction he needed.

"What do you say we go right now? Then we can come home and surprise the boys."

When we came back from the bike shop, Peter's car was in the driveway. Angus shook his head in amazement when he saw the bike. "Oh, T., a pink two-wheeler?" But he helped her buckle on her helmet and lifted her onto the seat. I ran inside and got the camera and snapped away as Taylor, proud in the bike seat, wobbled onto the sidewalk.

When I went to the house to get another roll of film, the phone was ringing.

Jill Osiowy sounded excited. "Something interesting's come up in the Little Flower murders, Jo."

I sank into the chair by the phone. I didn't want to hear what Jill was going to tell me. I didn't want to hear anything more about young women who had died before they'd even started to live.

"Listen to this," she said. "The cops have decided that Bernice Morin's death wasn't one of the Little Flower murders. The face wasn't mutilated, and the weapon was wrong. The other girls were stabbed with heavy knives, the kind you buy in a sporting goods store if you're going hunting. The scalpel that killed Bernice came from a medical supply house. It's the kind they use in hospitals and labs. I'll tell you the details later, but here's the scary part. The cops think Bernice's murder was a copy-cat killing. Think about that for a minute, Jo. There's somebody out there who figured if he made Bernice's death look like another Little Flower murder, the police would just kind of wink and look the other way. The perfect crime."

Suddenly, Jill noticed that I hadn't said anything. "Jo, what's the matter? Have you lost interest in these girls, too?" She sounded angry, and I felt a lump come to my throat.

"Don't be mad," I said. "It's not that I don't care. It's just . . . Jill, we've had a tragedy ourselves. Peter's friend Christy Sinclair died last night out at the lake. I'm doing my best to keep everybody, including me, from falling apart. I don't think I can take in another thing."

Jill's voice was soft with concern. "Jo, I'm sorry. How awful. Is there anything I can do? If you want company, I can be over there in ten minutes."

"Maybe later on tonight," I said. "Right now, I think we're better off on our own. Everybody's pretty fragile."

"I can imagine," she said. "Look, if you need me, call. You know, sometimes the best thing to do is just go through the motions."

And that's what the kids and I did. We went through the motions. All things considered, we didn't do badly. We had lunch, and the kids rode bikes most of the afternoon. No one broke a bone, and they were still speaking to one another when they came in for dinner. Peter curled up on the couch and watched the Mets-Dodgers game, and I put in bedding plants. I had just finished planting the last of the geraniums in the front garden when the police car pulled up.

I recognized Constable Perry Kequahtooway, but I didn't remember seeing the woman who was with him. She was a small brunette with a tense body and clever eyes. Perry Kequahtooway introduced her as Officer Kelly Miner.

"I wonder if we could step inside for a moment, Mrs. Kilbourn?" she said. "We're still puzzled about Christy Sinclair's next of kin situation."

They followed me in, and we sat down at the kitchen table.

Constable Kequahtooway spoke first. His voice was as gentle as his manner, but he got right to the point.

"We keep coming back to you, Mrs. Kilbourn. Everywhere we check – her employment records, her university insurance policy, even the form she filled out when she had some outpatient surgery in Saskatoon last February – every place we look, Christy Sinclair listed you as her next of kin."

I started to say something, but he held his hand up to stop me. "There's more. The Saskatoon police just checked out Christy Sinclair's condominium. Were you ever there?"

I shook my head. "She always came to our place."

"It's in Lawson Heights," Officer Miner said, "very posh. But the point is that there were pictures of you and Christy all over the place." She was watching my face carefully.

"Christmas pictures," I said.

"For the most part," she agreed.

"They'd have to be," I said. "Peter and Christy only dated for a few months, and Christmas was the only time we were taking pictures. But we took pictures of everybody during the holidays. There were pictures of Christy with all the people in our family."

"Not in her home," Officer Miner said. "And there weren't any indications of the Estevan connection you mentioned, either. No address book or envelopes with an Estevan address. We've checked in Estevan, too. No Sinclairs. No one by that name in the area. We're trying a picture ID down there, but so far no luck."

I looked at them both wearily. "What's your point?"

Officer Miner looked at me steadily. "Easy on there, Mrs. Kilbourn. There are no accusations being made here. This is an information session. We're just letting you know that, no matter how you saw the relationship, Christy Sinclair apparently chose you to be the most important person in her life."

Unexpectedly, I felt my eyes fill with tears. "It's too late now to do anything about that, isn't it?"

Officer Kequahtooway lowered his gaze and coughed. "Actually, Mrs. Kilbourn, it isn't too late. There are a number of details that have to be attended to, funeral arrangements, that kind of thing. You have no legal responsibility. I should make that clear. But there are other kinds of responsibility."

"Yes," I agreed, "there are."

Officer Miner stood to leave, and Constable Kequahtooway and I followed her to the front door. But when she started down the front walk, he didn't follow.

Instead, he turned and said, "Mrs. Kilbourn, this is unofficial, but I think when we get the final reports from pathology, we're going to find out that Christy Sinclair's death was a suicide."

I leaned against the doorjamb. "I kept hoping it wouldn't be," I said. "That makes everything a thousand times worse."

"It always does," Perry Kequahtooway said softly. Then he looked at me. "Sometimes people find comfort in searching out the truth about the life of a person who's passed on."

"You mean investigating?" I said. "But you'll be doing that."

Constable Kequahtooway shrugged. "That's right, we will, but sometimes people like you can get to a different kind of truth than the police do. It's just a thought, Mrs. Kilbourn. But I think, in the long run, it might comfort you and Peter to find out why you mattered so much to Christy Sinclair."

When he started down the steps, I touched his arm. "Constable, what does your last name mean? We had a friend years ago named Kequahtooway, and I know the name is significant."

He squinted into the sun, and then, unexpectedly, he grinned.

"In Ojibway," he said, "it means he who interprets. You know, the guy who tries to help people understand."

CHAPTER

5

On Victoria Day, when I went to the mailbox to get the morning paper, Regina Avenue was as empty as a street in a summer dream. I went in, made coffee and looked out at the backyard. Peter was in the pool swimming, and Sadie and Rose, our dogs, were sitting on the grass watching.

I went out and knelt by the edge of the pool.

"How's it going this morning?" I asked.

Peter swam to the edge of the water and looked up at me.

"It's been better," he said, and I could hear his father in the weary bravado of his voice.

"I know the feeling," I said.

His face was a mask. "I didn't go after her, Mum. When she said she was going out on the lake, I was relieved. I was going to have a whole hour where I didn't have to worry about her. So I didn't go after her, and she died. How am I going to live with that?"

"I don't know, Peter," I said. "But for starters, you can see that what you did was pretty normal. You thought about yourself. You wanted some breathing space, and when the chance came, you took it. Mother Teresa may not have done what you did, but most people, including me, would have. Look, I'm not saying that it was right to let Christy go when she was that upset, but we don't carry a crystal ball around with us. You didn't know what Christy was going to do, and you're certainly not responsible for what she did."

"Mum, listen to yourself. You don't even believe what you're saying. You know I didn't have to be in the boat with her. You know it's not that simple because you're the one who told me it's never simple – that we're always responsible for what we do and what we don't do. You've been drumming that into me for nineteen years, you can't expect me to just walk away now."

He pulled himself up on the side of the pool. His body, still pale from winter, was as graceful as his father's had been.

"I'm seeing Daddy everywhere in you today," I said.

He raked his hair with his fingers. "That's not bad, is it?"

"Not bad at all," I said. "Come on inside, and I'll get us some breakfast."

Taylor and Angus were already at the breakfast table having cereal. Taylor was unnaturally quiet. The night before when I had told her about Christy's death she had listened attentively, then gone off to her room to draw. When I went in to say goodnight, she was asleep, and the bedspread was covered with pictures of swans.

While Peter went upstairs to dry off and change, I poured us all juice and started batter for pancakes.

"Anybody want to take the dogs for a walk after breakfast?" I asked.

"Samantha's mum is taking us for a ride on the bike path," Taylor said.

"Are you up for that, T.?" I asked. "You just started yesterday."

"Samantha's mum has never ridden a bike in her life, but she says today's the day."

"Good for her," I said. "Angus, how about you?"

He wiped his mouth on the back of his hand. "I'm playing arena ball as soon as I'm through here, then I'm coming home to make a cake."

"A cake," I said, trying to keep the surprise out of my voice.

"Alison next door made this cake, and it was great. She says it's a real no-brainer."

"A no-brainer?" I asked.

He looked at me kindly. "Easy? Any dummy can do it?"

"Right," I said.

After breakfast, Peter and I put the dogs on their leashes and walked them downtown to Victoria Park. The walk to the park was a family tradition on the twenty-fourth of May weekend, one of those small ceremonies whose only justification was that we did it every year. My husband, Ian, used to say it was our way of making sure that Good Queen Vic, the fertility goddess, would smile on our garden.

It was the first really hot day of the year, and the streets were coming to life with people riding bikes or jogging or pushing babies in strollers. There was a regatta on Wascana Lake, and from the bridge we could see the bright sails of the skiffs waiting for wind.

Peter and I didn't say much. We never did. We sat on the bench in front of the statue of Sir John A. Macdonald and listened to the chimes the multicultural community had donated to the park play "Edelweiss." Four days earlier I had sat on this same bench with Mieka, reeling from the shock of the death of another young woman. It was not a pattern I was happy about repeating.

Finally I said to Peter, "Do you remember Constable Kequahtooway? He was the first one there the night of the accident."

Peter nodded.

"Well," I went on, "he says that taking care of the details of Christy's funeral and finding out more about her might help us accept what's happened."

"Face it," Peter said angrily. "Nothing's going to help."

He leaned back on the bench and raised his face to the sun. The chimes finished "Edelweiss" and started on "The Blue Bells of Scotland." When "Blue Bells" was finished, Peter leaned forward and looked across the park.

"That doesn't mean we shouldn't try to do the right things for Christy," he said. "But it's not going to be easy. Sometimes I wonder if she ever told me the truth about anything."

"Maybe that's what she wanted to tell me that last night," I said.

Peter shook his head. "You never give up, do you?"

"That's what your dad used to tell me. He didn't see it as a particularly admirable trait." I shrugged. "Anyway, the truth must be somewhere. I guess the place to start is Christy's family. The Estevan angle doesn't seem to be true, but she must have somebody. It's terrible to think of her people out there not knowing. How would you feel about calling some of Chris's friends in Saskatoon and seeing if she ever mentioned anything about her family?" I looked at him. "Nothing's come back to you, has it? I mean something she said that might help the police."

"Mum, she said so many things . . ." He leaned forward and put his arms around the neck of our golden retriever. The dogs had always been his consolation. In a minute he stood up.

"We'd better get back," he said. "I think what I'll do is drive up to Saskatoon. If I leave now, I can be there after lunch. It'll be easier for me to talk about Christy face to face. I'm hopeless on the phone."

"I know," I said, picking up Rose's leash. "I've talked to you on the phone for nineteen years."

As soon as we got to the house, Peter filled a Thermos with coffee and headed north. I was watching Angus line up the ingredients for his cake when the phone rang.

The man's voice was brusquely authoritative. "Joanne Kilbourn? This is the pathology department at Pasqua Hospital. We're ready to release Christy Sinclair's body and we need a signature." He hesitated, and when he spoke again he sounded almost human. "You'd better make some arrangements for a pickup."

I watched Angus carefully break three eggs into a cup, then I went upstairs and opened my closet door. I looked at the bright cotton skirts and blouses and wondered what you were supposed to wear when you signed for a body. I picked the dress closest to me, a grey cotton shirtwaist. As I left the house I caught my reflection in the hall mirror. I looked a hundred years old, which was about half as old as I felt.

What happened at the hospital was either Keystone Kops or cosmic justice working itself out. It began when I saw the picket line blocking the entrance. There was a nurses' strike in our province. Under normal circumstances I would have walked twenty miles before I crossed a picket line, but these were not normal circumstances.

A blonde woman, X-ray thin and carrying a picket sign, stood between me and the front steps of the hospital.

"I don't want to do this," I said to her, "but there's been a death."

"I'm sorry," she said and she lowered her sign. It said, "The Only Good Tory Is a Suppository."

The hospital was quiet. The administration had dismissed as many patients as possible before the strike. "To stream-line the operation," they had said. There was one harried-looking woman sitting in a reception area designed for four.

"Pathology," I said to her.

"Top floor," she said without looking at me.

When I got off the elevator, I was struck by how pleasantly domestic the pathology department seemed. There were plants everywhere. To the left of the elevator was a floor-to-ceiling window that filled the area with warm spring sunshine; to the right there was an area that looked like a nursing station. On the counter a huge azalea bloomed unseen by anyone but me. The nursing station was empty.

I walked to the window and looked out. Beneath me was Queensbury Downs, the racetrack, seductive as a sure thing in the May sunshine. Trainers were taking horses through their paces, and I could see the lines of the horses' powerful muscles as they moved around the track. I felt myself relaxing.

There was a cough behind me. When I turned, I saw a woman standing behind the counter. She was wearing street clothes, not a uniform, and she seemed as harried as the woman downstairs had been.

"Well?" she said, and her voice was flat and uninterested.

"Joanne Kilbourn for Christy Sinclair," I said.

"Right," she said. She turned, took a file from a rack on the wall and placed it on the counter between us. The name "Sinclair" was written in bright green felt pen across the top of the folder.

"Everything's ready for your signature," she said and opened the file. Behind her a phone rang. She answered it, looked even more harried, then ran down the hall. I picked up the form on the top. I thought I could sign it and have it ready when she came back. Cheerful as pathology was, I didn't want to stick around.

Underneath the release form was a typewritten report labelled "Autopsy Findings." I pushed it away from me. Then I looked at the bulletin board behind the nurses' station. Someone had tacked up a computer printout; the letters were large, mock-Gothic: "We speak for the dead to protect the living."

Good enough. I pulled the autopsy report toward me and began reading. The first page confirmed what Perry Kequahtooway said it would confirm: Christy Sinclair's death was a result of a deadly combination of alcohol and tranquilizers. The drug names and the strength of the pills didn't mean anything to me; obviously whatever Chris had taken had been enough to do the job. As I turned to the next page, I was surprised to see that my hands were shaking.

I found what I was looking for on page three. The typewriter pathology used had a worn ribbon, and the report was dotted with vowels whose imprint was so vague their identity could only be guessed at. Moreover, the report was written in the language of medicine, and I was a layperson. But I had given birth to three children, and there were certain things I knew. I knew, for example, that any woman whose reproductive system had been as badly scarred by repeated non-clinical abortion procedures as Christy Sinclair's had been was unlikely to sustain a pregnancy. I looked at that hard medical language again. No mention of a fetus, no mention of any physiological changes that would indicate pregnancy. There was no baby. I was flooded with relief and then, almost immediately, I was overcome by a sense of loss.

I replaced the first page, and that's when I saw it. About a third of the way down the page under the heading "Identifying Marks" was a single entry: "left buttock, tattoo, 3 cm, bear-shaped, not recent."

I felt my head swim. The harried woman came back. I signed the form and pushed it toward her without a word. I stood up and started to leave. She called after me. "You should make some arrangements to have her taken to a funeral home," she said. "You can use my phone, if you like."

She was, I knew, trying to be kind, and I walked into the nursing station.

"Just pick one and dial," she said pointing to her desk pad. Under the plastic were the business cards of all the funeral homes in town. Easy reference. I picked the one nearest our house and made my call. The woman went through the doors marked "No Admittance." I picked up the phone again and called long distance information.

Constable Perry Kequahtooway didn't sound surprised to hear from me, and he didn't chide me for reading a confidential file. When I told him about the teddy bear tattoos on the buttocks of two girls dead within a week, he whistled softly. "Now I wonder what that means?" he said in his gentle voice.

As I drove along the expressway, I repeated the question to myself. By the time I walked in the front door of my house, I still hadn't come up with an answer.

Taylor was sitting at the kitchen table eating cake. Her face was dirty except for the places where tears had run down her cheeks. A half-dozen *Sesame Street* Band-Aids were plastered on her knee. Angus was across from her.

When Taylor saw me, she said, "I wiped out."

"So I see," I said.

"I put the Band-Aids on myself."

"Right," I said. "Taylor, did you clean the cut out before you put on the Band-Aids?"

"No time," she said.

"Finish your cake and we'll make time," I said.

"I told you," Angus said wearily.

Cleaning Taylor's knee and disinfecting it was a trauma for us both. When we were through, we collapsed on the couch in the family room. Taylor snuffled noisily beside me, and I pulled her close. I looked at the sun shimmering on the brilliant blue of the pool and tried to block out the ugliness of the medical profile the coroner's words had drawn.

Christy Sinclair had had so many abortions she was sterile. There had never been a baby. Beside me Taylor sang a tuneless song and finally drifted off to sleep. Not long afterwards, I followed her.

When I woke up, Mieka was there with Greg.

"Phone call from the uncle," she said, "wanting to take you out for dinner. I accepted for you. Greg and I will take the kids to McDonald's and the movies so you can make a night of it." She looked at me. "I think we all deserve a night off, Mummy."

I looked at them groggily. "I don't think so, Miek. I'd be rotten company tonight."

Greg came and sat by me on the couch. "It'd do you good, Jo. You've had a hell of a time the last few days. We all have. Anyway, don't decide right now. Let's all have a swim. It's gorgeous out there. If you don't feel better after that, I'll call my uncle and tell him Mieka the Matchmaker will go out for dinner with him, and you can come to McDonald's with me and the kids."

By the time I came out of the pool, I'd decided against McDonald's. The mindless rhythm of swimming had always relaxed me. By seven o'clock, my heart still felt leaden, but I was ready. Mieka had suggested I find something sensational to wear. I didn't have anything sensational, but I did have a cotton dress that was the colour of cornflowers. Every time I wore it, good things happened.

As I met Keith at the front door, I hoped good things were going to happen again.

"No car?" I said.

"This place is in walking distance," he said. "Actually, it's my house. Our housekeeper got some food together and left. The rest of the evening is going to be a clumsy seduction scene. You can bolt out the door whenever you want."

"I'll let you know," I said.

The streets were quiet, and the air was sweet with the scent of flowering trees: chokecherry, lilac, crabapple.

At the corner of Albert Street there was a cherry tree in full bloom. We stopped under it and looked up into branches heavy with rosy blossoms, thin as silk.

"I feel like I'm standing in the middle of a Chinese water-colour," Keith said.

Just then a gust of wind came and the cherry blossoms drifted down on us, pink and fragrant.

I reached over and brushed the petals from his shirt. "Is this part of the seduction?" I asked.

He smiled. "Is it working?"

Suddenly I felt awkward. "Keith, it's been years since I've done this. There hasn't been anybody for me since Ian died."

He shrugged. "I'm not a teenager. I'm fifty-three years old. I've learned how to wait."

Keith lived in a two-storey apartment house on College Avenue. It was white stucco with a red tile roof, vaguely Spanish and immaculately kept up.

"Second floor," Keith said and we walked up an oak stair-case, opened the front door and went in. It was a comfort-able-looking apartment, airy and cool, with chairs and couches that looked as if they were meant to be sat in, gleaming hardwood floors covered here and there with hooked rugs, and a scarred pine table set for two in front of doors that opened onto the balcony.

Keith looked at me. "I'm not a cook," he said, "but don't worry. My housekeeper says everything's ready. I just have to follow her instructions about what to heat up and what to leave alone. Dead simple, she says."

"My youngest son would call it a no-brainer."

He grinned. "He'd be right. Would you like a drink first?"

"Gin and tonic would be great," I said. "It's been a rotten day."

Keith brought the drink. "Do you want to talk about it?" he asked.

I shook my head.

"In that case," he said, "why don't you have a look around while I follow my instructions."

"Need help?" I asked.

"Relax," he said. "Have a look at the art. It's my one extravagance. All Saskatchewan, you'll notice."

"So I see," I said. On the coffee table a Joe Fafard ceramic bull, testicles glowing like jewels between his flanks, sat proudly beside clay six-quart baskets filled with brightly glazed vegetables: potatoes, carrots, tomatoes.

"Victor Cicansky," I said looking at the vegetables. "My dream is to have a kitchen filled with these some day." On the walls an Ernest Lindner watercolour of a peeling birch hung next to a brilliantly coloured blanket painting by Bob Boyer. Over the mantel was a magically realistic painting of a horse, so black it seemed blue, leaping into the arc of the prairie sky. Underneath was a title plate: "'Poundmaker Pegasus' by Sally Love (1947–1991)." Sally was Taylor's mother. I was standing looking at the painting, remembering, when Keith came, slipped his hand under my elbow and said, "Come on, I'll show you the rest of the place."

He led me into a room that looked like a working office. There was a desk that Keith said had belonged to his father covered with files and papers, shelves of books and a wall full of political pictures. I moved closer to the pictures. They were all there, my chamber of villains, the men and women I had spent much of my adult life trying to turn out of office. Blaine Harris was in some of the pictures; Keith was in all of them, smiling with presidents and prime ministers and premiers. All the pictures were inscribed affectionately and fulsomely.

In the lair of the enemy, I thought.

Keith touched my arm. "Was this a mistake?" he asked.

"No, not a mistake," I said. "Just a reminder. What is your status these days, anyway? I remember hearing that you came back to Saskatchewan because you wanted time away from Ottawa. Is it just a summer holiday or a permanent thing?"

He shrugged. "It depends, I guess."

"On what?"

"I don't know. Just stuff. Come on, let's get out of here. It's killing the mood. Besides, I'm hungry."

"Me, too," I said. "Would it be rude to ask what we're having?"

"Probably," he said, "but you're with a friend, so you get an answer. Cold lake trout, some sort of green salad, cornbread and Chablis." He dropped a disc into the CD player, and the room was filled with the shimmering sounds of the Goldberg Variations. Keith held out his hand to me. "And Glenn Gould is going to play until we decide we've had enough."

"Which will be never," I said.

"Which will be never," he agreed.

We brought the food to the table, and he lifted his glass to me.

"To music," he said.

I sipped my wine. "Good," I said. I tasted the fish. "In fact, more than good. Everything's wonderful. Do you know this is only the second seduction meal of my life? When I was sixteen, the boy across the street invited me for dinner. His parents had left him alone overnight for the first time. I guess the temptation was too much. He made the most romantic evening – vodka and orange juice and candlelight and his mother's tuna fish casserole and, of course, music.

Guess what he played during dinner?"

"'Bolero,'" Keith said.

"That was later," I said. "During dinner he played 'Rhapsody in Blue.'"

Keith smiled. "What happened?"

"He told me about George Gershwin's tragically short life, trying, I guess, to impress me with the need to gather our rosebuds while we could. And I drank my screwdrivers and ate my tuna casserole and cried like a baby, because George Gershwin died so young and because I wasn't used to vodka."

"And then?" Keith asked.

"And then he walked me home. It was 1961. People took virginity seriously in those days. He ended up studying math and physics at U. of T. Last I heard he was a high-school teacher."

"I'm too old for a change of career," he said.

"I'll bear that in mind," I said.

Dinner was wonderful, and I could feel the darkness lifting. Keith Harris was easy to talk to, and it was fun to trade stories about political battles. When we were finished, Keith said, "Do you like Metaxa? I have a bottle I brought back from Greece for a special occasion. Let's have a little and I'll put on the wisest piece of music I know."

He took Gould's 1955 recording of Goldberg out of the CD player and dropped in another CD. "This is the version of the Goldberg Gould did in 1981," Keith said.

We took our Metaxa out on the balcony. Across the park, the lights from the legislature shimmered in Wascana Lake. The air was cool and smelled of fresh-cut grass and damp earth. We sat side by side in the stillness and listened as Glenn Gould played Bach. The interpretation was very different, not brilliant and risk-taking, but mature, rich and thoughtful. It was the work of a man who had learned a few things about life and about death. Good music to make love to when you were closer to the end of life than the beginning. I felt the familiar stirrings of sexual desire, and moved closer to Keith.

"Ready?" he said softly.

"I think I am," I said.

He took my hand and together we walked down the hall to his bedroom. Suddenly, I was unsure. I walked across the room and looked at the framed photographs on Keith's wall. They were unmistakably pictures of the north: the sun boiling on the horizon while the pines reached dark fingers into the red sky; a wood grouse standing one-legged on a piece of driftwood floating in shimmering water; a close-up of wildflowers growing through dead leaves.

"Beautiful," I said.

Keith came and stood beside me. "Blue Heron Point," he said. "I'm the photographer. I'm not exactly Alfred Stieglitz, but with the north as a subject, you don't have to be. I have a place up there. It's not much, just a cottage on the lake."

"A squeaky screen door and sand on the floor and dishes that don't match?" I said.

Keith smiled. "And a wood stove where you can boil your coffee and fry your eggs too hard and a woodbox filled with old *Saturday Night*s. Best of all, it really is away from everything. Not like that palace of Lorraine's on Echo. But I guess she had enough of the north growing up. Anyway, sand and squeaks and all, I love it."

"Angus is going to camp at Havre Lake in July," I said.

"Good, let's take him up together, and we can stay at the lake."

"Just like that?" I asked.

He looked at me. "Yeah. Remember George Gershwin. No use waiting around."

"Right," I said. Keith took me in his arms, and I felt as if the broken parts of me were coming together. When he caressed my breasts and kissed the hollow of my neck, the darkness that had been hanging over me lifted.

I kissed him. "Remember that Marvin Gaye song 'Sexual Healing'?" I said.

Keith's hands slid over my hips. "I remember."

"I'm beginning to believe in it," I said.

When the telephone rang, shrill and insistent, we looked at each other.

"Damn," said Keith. "Do you want to let it ring?"

"Yes, but I'd be worried all night it was one of my kids."

Keith picked up the receiver and said hello. He listened for a while then he said, "Just keep him quiet. I'll be right there."

Keith turned to me, "My emergency, not yours. Apparently, Blaine was trying to get up and he fell. I'd better go down and have a look. Why don't you come along?"

"I don't think I feel like going anywhere," I said.

"It's just downstairs," he said.

"Downstairs here?" I asked.

"Yeah, I thought you knew. This building is sort of a family place. Lorraine owns it and she has the bottom floor. I have this. And since my father had his stroke, he and the nurse who takes care of him have stayed in the apartment at the back. It's been great, really – he has his privacy but we're close."

We walked downstairs and knocked at the door at the end of the front hall. A man in his mid-twenties wearing sweatpants and a very white T-shirt answered. He had the powerful shoulders and upper arms of someone who worked out. Keith introduced us, and the man, whose name was Sean Gilliland, shook hands with me, then turned to Keith.

"Your father got out of bed and fell," he said. "I'd bathed him and brought his bedtime snack and we watched the news together. Then I turned out the lights and came into the living room. I was doing my stretch and strengthens when I heard this crash. I went in and he was on the floor. Mr. Harris, he'd been trying to make a phone call."

Keith looked at him incredulously. "A phone call?"

Sean shook his head. "I know. But that's what he was doing. He was over by that little table with the telephone. He must have dragged himself over on the furniture. He still had the receiver in his hand when I found him."

As we passed through the living room, I glanced at the TV. The sound was turned off; on the screen, six men as muscular as Sean were silently working on their abdominal muscles.

Blaine's room was cool and dimly lit. I stayed in the doorway and Keith went to his father. The old man looked pale and shaken; even across the room I could see the ugliness of the purplish knot rising on his forehead. Keith talked to his father for a while, soothing words I couldn't hear, and Blaine seemed calm. Then he saw me.

As soon as he caught sight of me, the old man tried to push himself up to a sitting position. All the while he was pushing himself, he was trying to talk. The sounds that came out were garbled and desperate. Finally, he got out a single word, "Killdeer." As soon as he said the word, he fell back on the bed exhausted. But his eyes never left my face.

"Killdeer?" I said. "Do you mean my name, Kilbourn?"

He began to push himself up again. Sean came over to me quickly. "Would you mind staying in the other room? Mr. Harris isn't supposed to get upset."

I went into the living room. Keith came out almost immediately. He put his arms around me. "I'm going to call the doctor. Do you want to go upstairs and wait for me?"

I shook my head. "I think I'll take a cab home. The day seems to have caught up with me."

He kissed my hair. "Damn," he said. "This evening shouldn't end with your going home alone." He smiled. "Jo, if I can find a copy of 'Rhapsody in Blue,' will you give me another chance?"

"I'll bring the tuna casserole," I said. "Call me later and let me know how your father is."

Keith called the doctor and then he dialled a cab for me. While I waited for it, I watched the strong young men on the television stretch and strengthen their already perfect bodies.

When I got home, Mieka was sitting at the kitchen table in her nightgown working on her business accounts.

"Can I retire yet?" I said.

She made a face. "Not unless you have a source of income I don't know about."

"Is it going to be okay?" I asked.

Mieka smiled. "It's going to be fine. Lorraine's going to set up a line of credit for me on Monday."

"She's really good to you, isn't she?" I said.

"I don't know what I'd do without her, Mum." Mieka took off her glasses. "Are you warming to her at all? I know she's not the kind of woman you cozy up to, but you know, Mum, she hasn't had an easy life. She kind of manipulated the wedding with Greg's dad, and I think she got more than she bargained for. Alisdair had pretty well gambled away all their money by the time he died, and Lorraine had a little boy to support. She's had to work hard to get where she is."

"I didn't know that," I said. "I knew Greg was just a baby when his father died, but I always thought it was the Harris money that kept things going there."

Mieka shook her head. "All Alisdair Harris left Lorraine and Greg was that place on the lake, mortgaged to the hilt, and a lot of angry creditors. Old Mr. Harris just about went broke himself trying to pay off his son's debts. Keith tried to help, but Lorraine insisted she could do it on her own. And you know, Mum, when she was getting started in real estate, women had to be . . ." She hesitated.

"Men pleasers?" I said.

"Yeah, I guess. Lorraine still talks about having to use her womanly wiles. But to be fair to her, the kind of men you knew at the university and even in politics were more enlightened than some of the men Lorraine had to deal with. She's done very well for herself, you know."

"I know she has," I said. "And I intend to smarten up."

Mieka laughed. "See that you do. How was dinner?"

"Wonderful," I said. "Anything I need to know about around here?"

"No. The kids had three Big Macs each and fries and milk-shakes, then Angus made himself a grilled cheese sandwich before he went to bed. There were a couple of phone calls for Peter. Jill called for you. She'll call tomorrow. I think that's it. Except for a prank call. Someone called and made weird noises and then dropped the receiver. Probably some meat-ball friend of Angus's."

"Probably," I said.

But I knew who had called, and I knew it wasn't a prank. I climbed the stairs and went into the bathroom to get ready for bed. I looked at myself in the mirror. I looked like a woman who had just about been made love to. I smiled at my reflection. Then I remembered, and I stopped smiling. What had Blaine Harris seen in my face? What was there about me that had made him drag himself along the furniture in his bedroom and risk his health to call me on the telephone?

"Killdeer," I said to my reflection. "Killdeer," and I turned away and went to bed.

CHAPTER

6

As I dressed for Christy's funeral the bedroom was dark. Since the early hours of morning, thunder had cracked and lightning had arced across the sky. Now the rain had come, steady and relentless. I smoothed the skirt of my black silk suit and checked my reflection in the mirror. The silver bracelet encircling my wrist gleamed dully – Christy's bracelet, now mine.

Three days earlier, Mieka had sent the keys to Christy's condominium to a friend in Saskatoon and asked her to go to Christy's place and choose a dress for her to be buried in. The woman had found a simple cotton dress the colour of a new fern; the price and the care instructions were still pinned to the sleeve. When Mieka brought it to the house to show me, I'd shuddered.

"Your great-grandmother always said that a green dress was bad luck."

Mieka had looked at me grimly. "I don't think Christy's luck could get much worse," she had said.

Christy wore the green dress. I dreaded seeing her at the funeral home, but it seemed to come with the territory when you were next of kin. Mieka and I drove over together the morning before the funeral. We were silent as we looked at Christy. Finally, Mieka reached over and touched the bracelet on my wrist.

"We should put this on her, I guess," Mieka said. "I never saw her without it until that last night."

"She wanted me to have it," I said.

"She did? But I thought . . ."

I turned it on my wrist so I could read the Celtic lettering. "Wandering Soul Pray For Me." In that moment, I felt the bracelet's power. Marcel Proust called these objects that are charged with independent life "Madeleine objects." Sensible people don't believe in such things, and I am a sensible woman, but from the moment I put it on, Christy Sinclair's bracelet was both a reminder and a spur.

I turned to my daughter.

"Mieka, would you mind leaving me alone with Christy for a moment?"

Mieka looked apprehensive.

"I'm all right," I said. "I just want to say goodbye."

She left, and very quickly I stepped to the casket and reached my hand under the small of Christy's back and half turned her. I pulled up her skirt. I could see the outline of the tattoo through the thin material of her panties, but still I had to know for certain. I pulled at the elastic waistband and slid Christy's underpants down. On her left buttock was the teddy bear tattoo. It was exactly the same as the tattoo I had seen on Bernice Morin the morning after she was murdered. I pulled the skirt down and turned Christy onto her back again.

"What does it mean, Christy?" I said. "What does it mean?"

We took two cars to the funeral. Peter was going with Mieka and Greg, and I was going with Jill Osiowy and Keith

Harris. When he phoned and asked what time he should pick me up, I had told him that he didn't have to be part of that sad day. His voice on the other end of the line had been matter of fact. "I'm interested in the long haul, Jo," he had said simply, and I'd thought that having Keith Harris with me for the long haul might not be a bad idea.

Planning the funeral had brought us face to face with all the unanswered questions of Christy's life. Who were the people who cared about her? Beyond a few colleagues at the biology lab, there didn't seem to be anyone. We had put a photo at the head of Christy's obituary notice in the Saskatoon and Regina papers, hoping that someone who had known her before would see it and come. But it seemed a slim hope, and we had chosen the smallest of the chapels at the funeral home to avoid the depressing symbolism of empty pews. What were her favourite flowers? Her favourite pieces of music? No one knew. Pete remembered a couple of songs she'd commented on when they'd been listening to the car radio, but they were songs for the living.

What, if anything, did Christy Sinclair believe in? She had never said. Greg went down to the library and came back with two pages of quotes about the endurance of the human spirit.

"Is there anything there we can use for a eulogy?" he asked after I finished reading them.

I shook my head.

"That's what I thought, too," he said. "My high-school coach said stuff like that when he sent us back into a game where we were really getting nailed."

"Thanks for trying," I said. "I've got an idea about something that won't sound quite so much like Vince Lombardi."

I pulled down my volume of Theodore Roethke and looked for the poem with the image of the pickerel smile that I had always connected with Christy. The poem was called "Elegy for Jane"; Roethke had written it for a student who had died from injuries when she was thrown from a horse. I copied the poem out, and it was in my purse the day I walked through the door of Helmsing's Funeral Home.

We had done our best. Still, as we filed into that tiny chapel with the empty pews and the tape of "Amazing Grace" whirring lugubriously in the background, there was no denying that Christy Sinclair's leave-taking of this world was going to be a pretty lonely affair. But as the tape changed to "Blessed Assurance," there was a stir.

Four young women had come in. Two were native, two weren't, but they all shopped at the same store: stiletto heels, stirrup pants tight as a second skin on their slender legs, nylon jackets with their names embroidered on the sleeve and crosses around their necks. They were, without exception, pretty, but their hair, gelled and curled, frizzed and sprayed, was too extravagant for their young faces, and their eyes were too wary for girls who weren't far along in puberty. They sat behind me. All during the readings I was aware of them; I could feel their presence, and I could smell the sweet heaviness of their hairspray, overpowering in the humid chapel air.

When it was time for me to read, I felt the familiar clutch of panic, but Keith smiled encouragingly and Christy's bracelet was warm around my wrist. I walked to the front of the room and took a deep breath. I had read "Elegy for Jane" many times in the past twenty-four hours. I knew it by heart. As I said the lines, I looked at Christy Sinclair's small band of mourners: at Jill Osiowy, head bowed, red hair falling forward to curtain her face; at Keith, whose eyes never left mine; at Greg, whose arm rested on my daughter's shoulder as if by his touch he could protect her; at my adult children, backs ramrod straight but sitting so close together you couldn't have passed a paper between them, reassuring one another as they always had that, no matter what, they had each other.

Behind them, the four young women listened to Roethke's words with closed faces. The final stanza of "Elegy for Jane" had always seemed to me to be heartbreakingly beautiful.

> If only I could nudge you from this sleep,
> My maimed darling, my skittery pigeon.
> Over this damp grave I speak the words of my love:
> I, with no rights in this matter.

As I recited the words, one of the girls began to cry.

She wasn't the only one. When I came to the last line of the poem, I was crying, too – for Roethke's Jane and for Christy Sinclair who had no one but me to speak the words over her grave.

The rain hadn't let up when we left the funeral chapel. There was a kind of portico outside the entranceway, and the young women were there in their thin jackets, looking up at the sky.

I went over to them. "Can we give you a lift anywhere?" I asked.

They stepped back from me as if I were an infection, but one of them, the tiny blonde who had wept during the poem, stood her ground.

"We're okay," she said.

I looked at her. Her peroxided curls were dark at the roots like Madonna's, and her skin beneath its heavy makeup had the telltale bumps of pubescence. There were streaks of mascara down her cheeks from her tears. I took a Kleenex from my bag and held it out to her.

"Your mascara has run a little," I said.

She grabbed the tissue and began scrubbing at the area under her eyes.

"Every time I wear this goddamn stuff, somebody makes me cry," she said.

"Same here," I agreed.

For a beat, the mask dropped, and she looked at me with real interest.

"Were you a friend of Christy's?" I asked.

The girl's face closed in on itself again, and she turned on her heel and stepped into the rain.

"Please, could we talk just for a moment?" I called after her.

She didn't look back. The others followed her, and I was left on the steps of the funeral home watching the four of them clip along Cornwall Street in their perilously high heels. The rain kept on coming, plastering their stirrup pants to their legs, soaking their thin jackets, bouncing impotently off the gelled curls and the hard-sprayed frizz of their elaborate hairdos. Finally, they turned a corner and vanished into the mist of the rainy city.

There are 180,000 people in Regina. Chance encounters are not unheard of here; still, running into Kim Barilko less than twenty-four hours after talking to her outside the funeral home seemed like a cosmic stretch.

I had dropped Taylor off at nursery school and come downtown to do a couple of errands. Later I was going to pick Taylor up, help Pete get organized for the trip to Swift Current, then meet Mieka and Lorraine Harris at the bridal salon for Mieka's first fitting on her wedding dress. A high-stress day.

I'd taken care of my business, and I was walking along Scarth Street toward the place I'd parked the car. The wet weather had continued. It was a grey muggy day, coast weather. There was a bridal shop on Scarth; in the gloom, its window, bright with paper apple blossoms and summer wedding gowns, was an appealing sight. I stopped to look. There was something surreal about all those mannequin brides in their virginal white. I could see my reflection in the window: a flesh-and-blood imperfect middle-aged woman in the midst of all that synthetic flawless youth. And then there was another reflection, just behind me: a young woman with the hips-forward slouch of a street kid and Madonna hair. I turned. For a split second she didn't notice me, and I was able to see her face as she looked at that fairy-tale dress. Her mouth curved with derision, but her eyes were filled with terrifying hope. I didn't want to see any more.

"Remember me?" I said. "We talked yesterday after Christy Sinclair's funeral."

She was wearing yesterday's stirrup pants and a sleeveless blouse the colour of an orange Popsicle; her lipstick was that same improbable orange, but frosted. A cross hung between her small breasts.

"I remember you," she said and she smiled. "You've got the same problem with Maybelline that I have."

There was a Dairy Queen next to the bridal shop. "Could we have a cup of coffee together – my treat?" I asked. "I'd like to talk about Christy Sinclair a little if it's okay with you."

She shrugged her thin shoulders. "Sure, I'm not going any-where. But her name was Theresa, not Christy."

"Theresa?" I said.

"Like in Terry," she said, "or the saint. If you hadn't put the picture in the paper we wouldn't have known it was her because of the wrong name." She opened her bag and pulled out the obituary. She tapped at it with an orange fingernail.

"That's Theresa," she said.

"What was her last name?" I asked.

The mask fell over her face again. "Look, I don't think I've got time for a coffee, after all."

"Can I drive you somewhere or just walk along with you?"

"It's a free country," she said, and then more kindly she added, "I have to get to the Lily Pad and help with lunch. It's my day."

"Is the Lily Pad a restaurant?"

She laughed, a short, unpleasant sound. "Yeah, it's a restaurant, a restaurant for people with no money."

"I'm sorry," I said.

"Why?" she said. "You don't have to eat there."

We both laughed, and when she began walking toward Albert Street, I fell into step with her. "My name's Joanne Kilbourn," I said.

"I'm Kim Barilko," she said.

She made good time, despite her stiletto heels.

"So," I said, "how did you know Theresa?"

"From home and then at the Lily Pad," she said. "She was going to be my mentor, but with my luck, of course, she goes and dies. I should have known better." Kim's lip curled with contempt at her gullibility.

"You're going too fast for me," I said. "Could you fill me in a little?"

"The Lily Pad is a place for runaways, street kids?" At the end of the sentence, her voice rose, and she watched my face for a sign of comprehension. When she saw what she was looking for, she continued. "They serve food and coffee and you can go there and watch TV or have a shower or just hang together. There's a lot of system stuff, crafts and counsellors and programs to help you learn a job. It's a hassle-free zone. Nobody's allowed to dick you around, not your parents, not your old man, nobody."

"Sounds good," I said.

She shrugged. "And there are mentors. Girls who have good jobs and great clothes and great lives, and they come in and talk to us and then they choose someone to kind of help along the way. Terry chose me, because she wanted to help a girl from home. Besides, she said she saw something in me."

"I can see it, too," I said. "Incidentally, how old are you?"

"Fifteen," she said.

A year older than Angus.

The Lily Pad was on Albert Street, not far from the city centre. It was an old house with the graceful lines of a building designed in the first years of the century. On the front lawn a wooden frog sunned himself on a lily pad. No words. On the grass and on the front steps, kids sat smoking. I had spent my life surrounded by children, but kids like these still tore at me. The dead eyes, the defiance, the sure knowledge that they were just putting in time before they entered their life's work as members of the permanent underclass. When I thought about what lay ahead of them, it was hard to believe we'd inched very far along the evolutionary scale.

They moved aside to let us pass as we went up the front steps, but whether we were there or not there was obviously a matter of indifference to them. Kim didn't comment about them or about anything. There was a bulletin board on the wall of the entranceway. Pinned to the top was a sign: "The Sharing Place." The board was empty. A door to what must have been the upstairs was blocked off by an old pine sideboard.

"Don't you use the upstairs?" I asked.

"No," Kim said, "they're afraid we'll set the place on fire. You know, from our unhealthy habit of smoking." She gave me a deadpan look. "When you're dealing with a dysfunctional population, you can't be too careful."

I didn't know what to say.

"That was a joke," Kim said. "Come on. I gotta get lunch started."

I followed her through a large front room filled with over-stuffed furniture that had obviously been rescued from a dozen different basements. In the corner Big Bird was singing about his neighbourhood on a large-screen TV. No one was watching. We walked down a dark hall to the kitchen. Money had been spent here. The floor shone, and the indus-trial-sized appliances were new and expensive. Kim went to the sink and washed her hands, then she took a slab of ham-burger meat from the refrigerator and threw it in an iron frying pan on the stove.

"Chili," she said. She began breaking up the meat with a fork. "I never knew anybody like Theresa in my life. She was like a person on TV, pretty and smart, and she had such great clothes, and that little red convertible of hers was so amazing." She jabbed at the still frozen centre of the ham-burger viciously. "Maybe she liked me because I admired her so much."

"There are worse reasons," I said.

The meat sizzled and Kim stirred it. A splash of grease flew up onto her Popsicle-coloured blouse.

"Shit," she said. "Shit on a stick." She looked at me sadly. "Theresa would never say anything like that. She was a lady like Julia Roberts in that movie *Pretty Woman*. I musta rented that video twenty times." Her voice fell. "Anyway, Theresa wanted to make me a lady, too."

Kim began opening tins of kidney beans and tomatoes and throwing them into the pan with the meat. She stirred the mixture with a wild, hostile energy.

"She told me she was going to teach me about clothes and hair, and we were going to talk about going back to school. She had this business and she was going to, like, train me . . ."

Behind me a voice, smooth, professionally understanding, said, "Kim, you know the rules about visitors."

The first thing I noticed about the man in the doorway was that he had the kind of unvarying mahogany tan he could have achieved only in a tanning salon. "Fake-and-bake tans," Mieka called them. In fact, he looked like a fake-and-bake kind of guy: he was about Keith's age, mid-fifties, but he was dressed like a fashion magazine's idea of a college kid, UBC sweatshirt, designer jeans, white sport socks, white cross-trainers. His hair had been professionally streaked, and whoever did it had done a better job than the hairdresser who did mine.

"No visitors in the kitchen, Kim," he said pleasantly. Then he turned his smile on me. It was as dazzling as the gold chain around his neck. "I'm sorry Kim forgot to share our rule with you."

"You run a tight ship," I said.

"We have to," he said.

Kim turned away without a word. Her face as she stirred the chili was impassive. She had withdrawn again. She was back in that detached and distant zone where nobody could dick her around. I touched her on the shoulder.

"Thanks for telling me about Theresa," I said. "I still can't get used to calling her that. I never told you my connection with her. She wanted to marry my son, and she felt very close to me. I never knew her."

Kim took a bag of chili powder from the cupboard and began shaking it into the pan. "You blew it," she said.

The man raised his eyebrows. "I think we should let Kim get on with her cooking. There are a lot of us looking forward to her famous chili. We all have our jobs here at the Lily Pad."

"What's yours?" I said.

Out of the corner of my eye, I saw Kim grin. I was glad she knew I was on her side.

His smile widened, but as he looked at me his eyes were appraising. "Why, I'm Helmut Keating, the co-ordinator," he said. "If you'd like to step into my office on your way out, I can share some information with you about how we operate here at the Lily Pad."

Behind Helmut's back, Kim carefully mouthed the word "*asshole.*" I nodded in agreement. Then I smiled at Helmut.

"Let's get in there and share," I said.

When I left, I was carrying a manila folder with some photocopied diagrams of the administrative structure of the Lily Pad and a half-dozen slick brochures to hand around to people I thought would be interested in making a contribution. "We rely on our friends," Helmut said smoothly as he walked me out the door and down the front steps.

It was a little after eleven-thirty. It was still muggy and overcast, and the kids were still sitting on the lawn smoking. None of them looked as eager to have their lives transformed as the attractive kids in the Lily Pad's four-colour brochure.

I drove to Taylor's playschool. She was waiting in the doorway with her teacher. When she saw me, she came running, and I felt a rush of pleasure. She was carrying a cardboard egg carton.

"Look," she said breathlessly. "The other kids started theirs before I came, so I was late, but teacher says it's never too late. Look at them. They all sprouted."

There were twelve bean plants in the dirt that filled the indentations.

"Do you know the story of Jack and the Beanstalk, Jo?"

"Maybe you could tell me while we plant those. If we hurry, we've got time before lunch. I thought we'd make something special. Pete's going back to his job today, remember?"

"Holding cows for the animal doctor," Taylor said seriously.

"Right," I said.

An hour later, beans planted, the kids and I were sitting down to gazpacho and warm sourdough bread. Pete had always been strong and resilient – "Peter is unflappable," his kindergarten teacher had written in a report-card comment that became a family joke. But that day as I watched him eat lunch, I wondered if there'd been too many blows. The visit to the people he and Christy knew in Saskatoon had been painful; the funeral had been worse. But it was the news that Christy had committed suicide that devastated him. He felt he was responsible, and nothing any of us said could convince him otherwise.

I didn't believe in keeping secrets from the kids. Most of the time, I thought it was best to know the truth and work from there. But as I looked at Pete across the table, pale and unnaturally quiet, I knew this wasn't most of the time. I decided not to tell him about my visit with Kim Barilko. And so we were both quiet, and I was glad Angus and Taylor were there to fill up the silences.

When Angus went back to school, Taylor went out to sit with her bean garden, and Pete and I were alone.

"I don't want to go back there," he said.

"I know," I said. "But it's the best thing. You'll be busy doing something you like, with people who didn't know Christy. And you'll be in those beautiful, beautiful hills. That's healing country down there."

He pushed his chair away from the table. "This'll put it to the test," he said grimly.

As his car turned the corner, I closed my eyes, crossed my fingers and prayed that time and distance would work their magic.

I could hear the phone ringing as soon as I went back in the house.

It was Jill. "Guess who just phoned me?" she said. "Bernice Morin's boyfriend."

"That little punk Darren Wolfe," I said.

Jill laughed. "That's a bit harsh for you, Jo."

"One of the cops who came to Judgements the morning Bernice died said it. I guess it just stuck in my mind."

"It's probably accurate enough," Jill said mildly, "but punk or not, Darren's in big trouble. He got arrested for Bernice's murder this morning. He says he's innocent, that somebody's framing him. Of course, guys like Darren are always being framed."

"How come he called you?" I asked.

"He needs money for a lawyer. He says the lawyers the court provides are either dykes or dweebs. He heard on the street that the network was working on the Little Flower case, so he's offered to give me the real story – in return for compensation, of course."

"Are you going to do it?"

"I can't," she said, "but I am going to talk to him. If he really is innocent, there are other ways to help him. Jo, I probably won't be able to get to see him till tomorrow, but I thought you might want to come along."

I thought, I don't want to do this. I don't want to step to the edge of the abyss again. Images flashed into my mind – the teddy bear tattoo on Bernice Morin's left buttock, the single entry under "Identifying Marks" in Christy's autopsy report – "left buttock, tattoo, 3 cm, bear-shaped, not recent." I knew I didn't have a choice.

"Yes," I said, "I'll come. Just let me know the time and place. I'll be there."

I hung up and walked to the kitchen window. Taylor was sitting cross-legged in her garden, looking at the place in the ground where she'd planted her beans. For a long while, I watched her. Suddenly, she looked at the window. When she saw me, her face was bright with happiness, and she jumped up and came running toward the house.

"I think they've already grown more, Jo," she said.

"We'll probably be able to have beans for supper," I said.

For a split second, she believed me, then she grinned. "Oh, Jo," she said wearily. "Another joke." She came over and put her arms around me. As I held her close, I remembered other times when it had happened just like this, times when, at the very moment when I was sure the darkness was going to swallow me, there would be a moment of pure joy. I kissed Taylor's ear.

"Come on," I said. "Time to get the bean dirt off. We have to go help some ladies sew Mieka into her wedding dress."

CHAPTER

7

When I awoke the morning after Peter left, my bedroom was filled with light and birdsong, good omens. The digital clock on my radio read six o'clock, early, but when I looked at the sun streaming in, the waking world seemed to have a lot to recommend it. I brushed my teeth, pulled on my swimsuit and went down to the pool. The dogs, ever optimistic, followed at my heels in case I decided to change course and take them for a run. I disappointed them, but it was worth it. When I dived into the pool, I felt the thrill of physical well-being, and after twenty minutes of laps, the heaviness of the day before had left my body, and I was full of hope.

It was, I decided, time to get back to work. Lost in the mountain of unpacked cartons in the garage was a box of newspaper clippings, political articles I had saved during the past year because they seemed worth thinking about again. I could start there. We were due for a federal election in the fall. I could write a book about the campaign from the provincial viewpoint. I switched from the breast stroke to the crawl. "Sky's the limit," I said. "All you need to do is start. The time is now." I pulled myself up on the side of the pool, ready to go.

Taylor was just coming out of the house. Her face was still rosy from sleep, and she was ripping off her pyjama top with one hand and trying to pull on her bathing suit with the other.

"I'm coming, Jo. Wait for me. I'll show you my dog-paddle."

She put her arms around my neck, and the ground-breaking book on the upcoming election was temporarily on hold. By seven o'clock, Angus had joined us and we were all sitting at the picnic bench in our bathing suits eating cereal. When he finished, Angus went in to watch the sports news on TV.

I turned to Taylor. "We've got time to do a little work before you go to school. Why don't you bring out your drawing stuff while I read the paper?"

She brought her sketch pad and her case of coloured pencils, always so carefully arranged and sharpened, sat down opposite me and began to draw. Today it was baseball players, and as I watched the blank page fill up with kids in baseball uniforms pitching and hitting and leaping off the page to catch a hard-hit ball, I was humbled by her ability. Even her face seemed to change when she made art. The ordinary little girl who couldn't sit still for a story or remember to flush the toilet was transformed into someone else, a disciplined person who loved her work and knew it was good. When Taylor was drawing, I could see her mother in the set of her mouth and in her stillness. It was a good feeling.

I still hadn't read the front page of the *Globe and Mail* when Jill called.

"Two things," she said. "One, we can see Darren Wolfe at nine o'clock this morning. Two . . . No, I'm not telling you about two till I see you. I want to watch your reaction."

It was a little after eight-thirty when Jill rang our front doorbell. She was wearing a white silk blouse, a navy blazer and grey slacks.

So was I.

"We look like the Bobbsey Twins," I said.

"Nah," Jill said. "One of the Bobbsey Twins was a boy. We're just fashionable – the faux prison guard look is really hot this spring."

When we turned onto the Albert Street Bridge, Jill said, "Are you ready for the big news?"

"As long as it's good," I said.

Jill laughed. "I think it is. How would you like to be one of the panellists on *Canada Today*?"

Canada Today was a new show Jill's network was trying over the summer months, nightly at seven, half an hour of national news, then half an hour of a political panel. There were five proposed panels, one from each region, one for each night.

"I thought that was all set," I said, surprised. "Wasn't there an article in the paper last week saying you were going with the presidents of the provincial parties?"

"That was last week," she said briskly. "Today the presidents are 'too narrowly partisan, too likely to be idealogues.' At least that's what the fax says. Today what we have in mind is Senator Sam Steinitz, Keith Harris, and you."

"God, Jill, let me catch my breath. That's pretty high-powered company. Am I there as the token female?"

"No, you're there as the token person with a progressive mind," she snapped. "Say yes."

"Yes," I said.

"Good," she said. "Listen, I'm going to produce the first few shows myself. The network's got big plans for this show. There's bound to be an election in the fall, and they think *Canada Today* could grab an audience. Not much of what we do here goes national, so I want to make sure this doesn't look like Aaron Slick from Punkin Crick."

"When do we start?" I said.

"June third. That's a week from Monday," she said. "Soon, I know, but you're a quick study. I'll have some specific topics for you by the weekend, but if you can't wait to get started you can spend the afternoon thinking about something general, like where you think the country should be heading."

"Whither Canada?" I said. "Hasn't that been done?"

"Not by you," Jill said.

"Okay, whither Canada it is," I said. "And Jill, thanks."

"For what?"

"For thinking of me."

"It wasn't me, Jo. When I went into my office this morning, there was your name. It had arrived miraculously, by fax."

"Miraculously from where?"

"On high," she said. "On highest. The fax came from the office of Con O'Malley himself. The president of the network."

"How would the president of NationTV know about me? Jill, doesn't this seem a bit weird to you?"

She shrugged. "Not so weird, Jo. Your publisher's in Toronto, right? He and Con were probably hoisting a few at the Boys' Club last night, and you know how these things work. This morning when somebody got the bright idea of changing the panel, your name was front and centre in Con's mind. He prides himself on being a hands-on guy. Being able to suggest a name in Saskatchewan is just the kind of thing that he'd get off on. Believe me, Jo, whatever the explanation is, it will be that simple. Now, relax and give yourself up to the pleasures of life in the fast lane of TV journalism."

We drove north along Winnipeg Street, turned right at the heavy-oil upgrader and rolled up our windows as we passed the city dump. When Jill's ancient Lincoln started bumping along the country road that took us to the Regina Correctional Centre, I tapped her on the arm.

"So this is life in the fast lane," I said.

I had been to the correctional centre before. I remembered it as a depressing and forbidding place. It still was. After we were cleared through security, a guard took us to the visitors' area. Everything about the room was uniform, drab, institutional. Everything, that is, except Darren Wolfe. He was waiting for us on the prisoner side of the Plexiglas divider, and he was one of a kind.

His blond hair was parted in the centre, and it fell almost to his waist. His eyes, eyebrows and the roots of his hair were black. A gold cross hung from his left ear. He wore black leather pants, skin tight, a black leather vest taut against his bare chest and a kind of Edwardian smoking jacket of red and black velvet.

"They let them wear their own clothes till after sentencing," Jill whispered.

"Just as well," I said. "I think Darren would be pretty lost without his plumage."

There was a speaker phone on our side of the Plexiglas, and as soon as we were all seated, Jill leaned forward and introduced me to Darren Wolfe. She said I was the mother of the woman who had found Bernice's body.

Darren looked at me without much interest. "Yeah?" he said. "That must've been a bad start to your daughter's day."

Ingratiating, saying what he thought I wanted to hear. I felt a chill.

"It was a tragedy for us all. From what my daughter said, Bernice was an interesting young woman."

"Yeah," he agreed, "she was that." He nodded his head, remembering. "She was her own worst enemy. She was just a kid when I met her, but she'd already hustled for a coupla years. That mouth a hers had got her thrown out of her last setup. They couldn't intimidate her."

I looked at the preening boy across the table from me, and my mind started to float. Bernice had gotten her prize tattoo the morning after he beat her up. She had endured three hours of agony to get a picture of unicorns etched into her upper back because unicorns were her totem; like her, they were too proud to get intimidated.

"Anyway, I didn't do her," Darren Wolfe was saying. He had turned his attention to Jill. Conversation with me was pointless; I couldn't get him a deal with the network.

He leaned forward so that his forehead was almost touching the glass divider. His mouth was sullen, and his eyes were angry. "They haven't got anything," he said. "I knocked her around a few times, but it wasn't personal. Jesus, everybody fought with that bitch. Anyway, I don't do girls." He looked quickly around the room to see who was there. Then he lowered his voice. "Look, the truth is, I haven't got any bodies."

"What?" I asked.

He looked at me, exasperated. "I haven't got any bodies." He moved closer and dropped his voice. "I've never killed anybody." Having confessed the worst, he was restored. He straightened up, and his mouth curled into arrogance. "So, Jill," he said, "I've got some things to say that you oughta hear."

For the next twenty minutes Darren Wolfe gave us a conducted tour through the world of the Little Flower murders. I felt as if I'd stepped through the looking glass. The world Darren described, casually violent, retributive, vicious, seemed in every way alien from my own. But it wasn't. The streets Darren Wolfe drove on in the course of his business day were the same streets I drove on; the street corners his girls worked were the street corners I walked past; the hotels and apartment blocks where they turned tricks were part of my landscape. By the time he finished, I was badly shaken, and he saw that.

One thing Darren Wolfe knew was women. He wanted me on his side, and he knew I wasn't. When Jill and I stood up to leave, he reached toward me, flattening his fingertips against the Plexiglas the way prisoners do in movies.

"Look," he said, "I know you think I should be all broken up about Bernice. I can live with that, but before you write me off, you've gotta understand one thing. Bernice wasn't like the kind of girls you know. Girls like Bernice, they ask for it."

"Girls like Bernice . . ." As I walked to the car, Darren Wolfe's dismissal pounded in my head. As I opened the door on the passenger side, I remembered another judgement. Hours before she died, Christy Sinclair had sounded the same chord of death, justice and dismissal: "When girls like Bernice die," she had said, her voice trembling, "it's just biological destiny . . . They're born with a gene for self-destruction."

Jill didn't say anything till we were pulling out of the prison parking lot. "Sorry you came along?" she asked.

"No," I said. "Just in a state of shock. How does a boy like that live with himself?"

"He sees himself as a businessman, Jo. Out there like the other guys, showing a little hustle, operating in accordance with the laws of supply and demand. I'll bet you a hundred dollars he sleeps like a baby."

"I'll bet his girls don't," I said. I was wearing the silver bracelet Christy had given me, and my finger traced the lines of the Celtic letters. "Wandering Soul Pray For Me."

"How do you break the cycle?" I said. "How can you make it possible for people to have good lives?" Kim Barilko's face, mascara-streaked, defiant, flashed before my eyes. "Every

time I wear this goddamn stuff, somebody makes me cry."
How many times, I thought. How many times had someone
made Kim Barilko cry?

I remembered the light in her eyes when she'd talked
about all the things Christy Sinclair was going to teach her.
Then I remembered the derisive curve of her lip as she
talked about how stupid she had been to believe anything
good could happen to her.

Fifteen seemed pretty young to be giving up on life. I
turned to Jill. "How would you like to be a mentor?" I asked.

"Yours, Jo? Finally admitting you need some guidance? I'd
be delighted. You can start by throwing out all those sensible shoes you're so fond of."

"I'll do that," I said. "But actually the person who needs
someone to be her teacher, guide and friend is a lot more
adventurous in her clothing than I am."

When I finished telling her about Kim Barilko, Jill didn't
hesitate. "I'd be honoured, Jo. I really would. But not today.
Listen, I've decided I'm going to really move on this Little
Flower case. I've tried to get Toronto to give me a budget for
this, but they say, with restraints and all, we should be doing
upbeat stories with wide audience appeal. 'Celebratory' was
the word my immediate superior used, I believe. Anyway,
give me the weekend to see if any of Darren's leads pan out.
First thing Monday morning I'll go over to the Lily Pad, and
we can get started."

"Jill, would you mind if I went over there after lunch and
talked to her? I hate to think of Kim going through the
weekend without some good news."

"Of course I don't mind. Maybe she'd like to come to my
office Monday. I could show her around and take her for lunch
in the cafeteria. Most kids get a kick out of watching the
people they've seen on TV eat their tuna fish sandwiches."

"Thanks, Jill."

"For what? Trying to redress the balance a little? Don't you think it's about time?"

I picked Taylor up at school. "Samantha's birthday party," she said as she got in the car. "It's today. Do we have a present?"

"Wrapped and on the dining room table," I said.

"What is it?"

"An onion tree. Every time Sam takes off an onion, two more will grow in its place."

Taylor looked into my face. "That's a joke, right?"

"That's a joke, right!" I said, and we both laughed.

After lunch I was in the front yard watering the geraniums when Taylor came out. She was carrying the birthday present, and she was wearing a pink party dress, her baseball shirt, baseball socks and runners.

"How would you like a mentor to advise you about your clothes?" I said.

She grinned at me.

I didn't fall for it. "T., you're going to have to change," I said. "Why didn't you wear what I put out for you?"

"Because I felt happy," she said.

It was the first time she had said that since her mother died. If I'd had a party dress and baseball socks handy, I would have worn them myself. I reached down and took her hand.

"Good enough," I said. "Let's go to Samantha's party."

After I dropped Taylor off, I drove downtown to the Lily Pad. Not much had changed. The wooden frog still sunned himself on the lawn, and the kids still smoked on the steps. When I walked past them, they looked at me incuriously through dead eyes. The front door was open and I went in. Someone had tacked up a sign on the Sharing Place: "Global

thought for the day: Have a birthday party for the world."
On the TV in the living room, Oprah was talking about rela-
tionships; no one was watching. I kept on going. The state-
of-the-art kitchen was gleaming and empty. On the counter,
what looked like twenty pounds of standing rib roast thawed
on a tray.

I was trying to decide what to do next when my friend
Helmut came in. I hadn't liked him the day before and I
didn't like him now. He was wearing a sweatshirt that said,
"Let Me Be Part of Your Dream." When he greeted me, his
smile was as dazzling as ever, but there was no mistaking
the hostility in his eyes.

I gestured toward the rib roast. "Good groceries," I said.

He moved between me and the meat. Incredibly, it seemed
as if he was trying to keep it a secret.

"Don't hide it," I said. "You deserve praise. Not many
drop-in centres for runaways serve prime rib."

"I thought I shared the rule about visitors the last time
you were here, Joanne," he said.

"You know my name," I said. "Who told you?"

The smile was even more forced. "I don't think that's
something you need to know."

"I think it would help us relate," I said. "Caring people
shouldn't have secrets from one another."

"Kim told me," he said.

Not in a million years, I thought. But I smiled at him.
"Well, Kim is the person I've come to talk to."

He gestured to the empty kitchen. "As you can see, she's
not here."

"Do you expect her back soon?"

Helmut shrugged. "The kids who come here are dysfunctional, Joanne. They aren't big planners. People come. People
go. It's called a transient population."

"What about your mentor program?" I asked.

I could see the muscles in his neck tighten, but his smile grew even wider. "That's one of our few failures. We had to abandon it. There were too many jealousies. Adolescent girls tend to be emotionally labile."

"Pretty sudden decision, wasn't it?" I said. "I'm sure Kim Barilko wasn't the only young woman who was looking forward to having a chance at a different kind of life."

Helmut Keating looked at me stonily. "We have programs here at the Lily Pad," he said, "as you would have discovered if you'd read the brochures I gave you."

"How can the programs help Kim when you don't know where she is?" I asked.

Helmut narrowed his eyes.

"Just asking," I said. "I don't think we're communicating very well here, Helmut. Maybe I'd better let you get that million-dollar roast in the oven. Is there someplace I could leave a message?"

"The Sharing Place," he said tightly.

I wrote a note to Kim, telling her that a friend of mine who worked in television was interested in meeting her, and I left my name and phone number. I pinned it right under "Have a birthday party for the world."

That night Keith called and we went to a new East Indian restaurant. We ate samosas and curried shrimp and groped at each other under the table. It was a nice evening, and it seemed to usher in a nice weekend. Saturday morning the kids and I enrolled Taylor in a summer art class at the old campus, then we went downtown and shopped for the endless items on Angus's camp list. In the afternoon, I sat on the deck and read political journals while Taylor and her friend Samantha splashed around in the pool.

Sunday evening I went to the shower Lorraine was giving

for Mieka. It was the first time I'd been inside Lorraine's Regina apartment. The floor plan was the twin of Keith's, but the decor was coolly modern – all white. The only touches of colour in the room were the silvery wrapping paper of the gifts piled high on the table beside the window, the pink of the sweetheart roses that bloomed from a crystal bowl beside the chair for the bride-to-be, and the ice-cream pastels of the dresses the guests were wearing.

It was an evening that unfolded itself impressionistically, in a series of flashes that somehow revealed the whole. The rosy pink of the cold lobster in the seafood salad was the same shade exactly as the chilled rosé Lorraine handed around in her delicately fluted glasses. Lorraine's friends, brilliantly fashionable, talked in throaty voices about new cars and old boyfriends or old cars and new boyfriends; no one seemed to care which. My daughter, who had always despaired of her looks, bloomed into beauty as she breathed in air perfumed by spring roses and listened to her friends' gently mocking talk of love.

There were other flashes, equally sharp but more unsettling: the faint shudder of distaste that ran through Lorraine Harris's body when she overheard Jill and me talking about my visit that day to the Lily Pad. Lorraine's eyes, stern behind her horn-rimmed glasses, as she laughingly warned me against raising unpleasant topics at my daughter's wedding shower. The two elegant women, friends of Lorraine's, who heard me mention Helmut Keating's name and came over to gossip about him and the Lily Pad.

"Of course, I'm on the board," said the first woman, "so I see a fair bit of Helmut. He's a bit too free with the jargon, but he works hard and the kids seem to love him. He's a very caring guy."

The second woman, who had had several glasses of rosé, roared. "And don't forget that fabulous streaking job. Now

whoever did that is an artist. I think there's a song there,"
she said. "Helmie has great hair and it's only fair 'cause he's
a very caring guy."

The first woman smiled and took her friend's arm. "Time
to say good night," she said. And they did.

And one last vignette. Just before the party broke up, there
was a knock at the door; it was Blaine Harris. I could see his
nurse, Sean, waiting in the hallway, but Blaine propelled his
own wheelchair across the room and handed Mieka a long
blue jeweller's box, tied with a white ribbon. Mieka opened
it, held the gold locket that was inside up for everyone to
see, then fastened the chain around her neck.

The old man watched intently, then made a saluting
gesture to Mieka and wheeled himself through the door into
the hall. The whole scene couldn't have taken much more
than a minute, but by the time Blaine Harris left, there
wasn't a dry eye in the room.

It was a nice moment, and as I walked home, warmed by
that memory and by other memories of the glowing party, I
decided it was time to stop worrying about the things I
couldn't change and to start cherishing the good things in
my life.

During the next week I tried. I read; I went over to the TV
station and watched tapes of politicians and press confer-
ences and pundits; I took Taylor to two art galleries to see
new exhibits; I shopped and made the final purchases on
Angus's camp list. I even bought a mother-of-the-bride dress
in aquamarine silk. Mieka was so relieved she took me out
for ice cream and a movie. It was a week in the life of a lucky
woman. And every night before I slept I could feel Christy's
bracelet burning warm on my wrist; every morning when I
stretched for the day, I could feel the bracelet's weight heavy
on my arm.

I found I made detours. I took not the shortest route between stops but the one that would take me close to the Lily Pad where I could run in and check the Sharing Place. "Have a birthday party for the world" gave way to "Wave to a bird because you cannot fly," then "Wake up early and dance for the sunrise," but there was never a message for me from Kim. Three times I went to the bridal store where I had come upon Kim by chance the day after Christy's funeral. I ached to see her. I ached to right the wrong I had done to Christy. I ached to redress the balance.

Monday, June third, I did the first television show. Keith picked me up and we drove to the studio together at five-thirty. We walked through the glass and steel lobby with pictures of the network stars suspended from the ceiling like the banners of medieval knights. A young woman, slender and fashionable in a black jumpsuit and odd socks, one pink, one turquoise, led us along corridors to an underground room where another young woman put makeup on us. She looked at Keith's solid pale-blue suit approvingly and flicked his face with a powder puff. When it was my turn, she said my makeup was pretty good. She did some deft things with eyeshadow. "Brown is always more natural looking," she whispered. She touched my earlobes with blush, then stood back and looked at me appraisingly. I had bought a new dress for the show, flowered silk, pretty as a summer garden.

"Next time," she said kindly, "try to find a solid colour. That's going to make you look like you're wearing your bedroom curtains." She looked at her watch, grinned and said, "Showtime. Knock 'em dead."

The young woman with the odd socks marched us through a corridor to the studio.

"I like your dress," Keith said.

"You'd like my bedroom," I said.

We got microphones, Jill introduced me to Sam Steinitz, who arrived breathless from the airport, and we were away. It seemed to go all right, but I was immensely relieved when it was over. When they took off the microphones, Keith turned to me and grinned. "Well, shall we go over to my place and debrief?"

We stopped at a French deli and bought crusty bread and cold cuts and a salad made of tomatoes, fresh basil and ripe Brie. Then we went to Keith's, debriefed and sat on the balcony eating dripping sandwiches, drinking wine and analyzing each other's performances. I decided I liked TV.

Keith drove me home around ten-thirty. Mieka and Greg were sitting at the kitchen table poring over the guest list. They gave me a standing ovation when I came in. I kissed Mieka and she made a face.

"Oh, why do I find myself suddenly thinking of Provence?" she said. "I don't suppose you brought leftovers."

I held up a greasy bag.

"You suppose wrong," I said. She and Greg attacked the bag like kids, and Mieka ran through the evening's messages. There were calls from old political friends, most of whom, according to Mieka, wanted to tell me what to say next time. Peter had called collect. He'd been in the middle of nowhere when the show came on, but had found a pub with a TV and made everybody watch his mother. He'd liked the show, and he said the guys in the bar thought I seemed sharp for a woman. My old friend Hilda McCourt called from Saskatoon to tell me I deferred to Keith and Sam Steinitz too much and that solid colours tended to photograph well and make the wearer look slim, but that she thought I had a future in TV. Keith and I had a final glass of wine with the kids, and by eleven-thirty, I was showered and in my night-gown. When I turned down the bedspread, I saw the picture

Taylor had left for me. It was called "Jo on TV." I was smiling and wearing my flowery dress. I looked very thin and very fashionable. When I went to tuck her in, I gave her an extra hug. That night I went to bed happy.

The next day I got a message from Kim Barilko.

CHAPTER

8

The morning of June fourth was glorious: hot, blue-skied, alive with possibilities. After I showered, I took the dogs for a run, got the kids off to school and sat down at the picnic bench with a cup of coffee. The tension of the first TV show was over; the kids were safe; the shoes I'd chosen to wear with my mother-of-the-bride dress were off being dyed. Life was under control. All I had to do was sit back and enjoy it. But I couldn't.

Half an hour later, wearing sandals, a black-and-white checked sundress and my Wandering Soul bracelet, I pulled up on the street in front of the Lily Pad. I walked up the sidewalk and made my way through the smokers on the front steps. By now they were used to me; I was as unremarkable to them as the wooden frog sunning himself on the lily pad on the front lawn. I went straight to the Sharing Place. My note was there, but there was still no answering message. As I walked to my car, I felt the familiar sting of defeat.

That's when I saw him. He was standing by my Volvo, slight, young, dressed to intimidate: sleeveless black shirt; skintight blue jeans, black hair pulled into a ponytail under a high-crowned black cowboy hat, black reflector glasses. He lit a cigarette and inhaled it lazily.

"I saw you on TV," he said. "It was on in the place where I was," he added quickly, in case he'd revealed something.

I could see myself reflected in his glasses. I seemed distorted. My forehead was huge, and my body seemed to dwindle off, caricaturelike, toward a point on the sidewalk.

"You're the one looking for Kim," he said.

My face in the shining black glass was suddenly alert.

"Yeah," I said. "I am."

"She'll meet you," he said. "Until last night she didn't believe it about you knowing someone on TV."

"Where can I find her?" I said.

"She'll find you," he said. "Tonight at the coffee shop in the bus station, ten-thirty." Then, for just a second, the tough-guy edge in his voice softened. "She's a good kid," he said. "She needs a lucky break."

I called Jill and told her the news. She sounded tired and discouraged.

"Maybe some good will come out of this after all," she said. "I'm certainly getting nowhere."

"Darren Wolfe's hot information wasn't so hot?" I said.

"Oh, it was hot, all right, at least I think it could be hot, but somebody needs to do a lot of digging, and the network is determined it isn't going to be us. I told you they were dragging their heels on this, so this morning I decided to fax Toronto all my notes from the interview with Darren. Jo, I was so sure if I just laid things out they'd see what a great story the Little Flower case is."

"And they didn't," I said.

"Twenty minutes ago I got a fax telling me in no uncertain terms that street journalism is not the network's mandate and that I'm the only regional news director who hasn't submitted plans for Canada Day coverage. Here I am sitting on one of the best stories of my life, and I have to shut everything down so I can call Eyebrow, Saskatchewan, and see what they're doing on July first."

I laughed. "I'll bet you a hundred thousand dollars they're having a softball tournament."

"No bet," she said. "Listen, Jo, see if you can shake anything loose from Kim tonight, would you? Specifically, about kids disappearing."

"You mean kids her age?"

"No, little kids."

I felt a chill. "Jill, what do you think's going on?"

"I don't know. I just get glimpses. Be careful, Jo. I'll tell you what I tell our interns from the school of journalism. Keep your eyes open, don't believe anything until you've heard it from three sources, tell only the people who need to know and always remember where the door is."

"Right," I said. I hung up and looked at my watch. It was going to be a long wait till ten-thirty. I went upstairs, made files for a box of clippings and started to organize my office. Busy work. At noon I picked up Taylor, and we drove downtown and offered to buy Mieka lunch at Mr. Tube Steak if she'd come and sit in the park with us. She did.

After lunch, Taylor and I had a swim and a nap and started to get ready for dinner. Keith was flying to Toronto that night, so I'd asked him over for an early barbecue.

Taylor and I made a potato salad and coleslaw. After she'd finished at Judgements, Mieka came by with a double chocolate cheesecake from another caterer. ("She's good, but I'm going to be better," she said, smiling, as she put the cake in the refrigerator.) Around five, Greg and Keith came over, and we barbecued chicken. It was a nice family evening. After coffee and dessert, I drove Keith to his place to pick up his bags. We walked upstairs together; when we opened the door, Keith's apartment was hot and airless.

"Air conditioner must have gone again," he said. "Do you want me to run inside and grab my bags? We can have a drink at the airport."

"Let's just sit out on your balcony," I said. "I've got some news about Kim Barilko, and I'd rather you were the only one who heard."

Keith took my hand and led me to the balcony. He was silent as I told him. When I finished, he looked at me searchingly. "Jo, are you sure you're not getting in too deep with all of this? The Hardy Boys stories are fun when you're a kid, but this sounds serious to me."

"Nancy Drew," I said.

Keith raised his eyebrows.

"For girls it was Nancy Drew," I said, "and I know it's serious, but, Keith, I can't just walk away. Kim Barilko isn't anybody's ideal fifteen-year-old, but she's funny and smart, and she deserves a chance not to be hassled by assholes."

"I take it that's a direct quote," Keith said.

"Pretty much," I said.

Suddenly there was a low moaning sound from the balcony below us. "Blaine's air conditioner must be broken, too," Keith said.

The air was split with hooting noises, and Keith smiled sadly. "Well, you are a miracle worker, Jo. Those are Blaine's approbation signs. He agrees with you. Blaine believes that Kim Barilko deserves a chance."

After I drove Keith to the airport, I came home, had a swim with the kids and got everybody settled for the night. Then I drove downtown. At ten-thirty I pulled into the parking lot opposite the bus station. Across the street at the Shrine Temple, men's laughter escaped through an open door into the hot night. The bus station was brightly lit. I went into the coffee shop, sat down at the counter and ordered iced tea. There was a Plexiglas wall between the coffee shop and the bus waiting room. I could see people sitting on benches, patient, still. Mostly they were native people or they were old. The past winter a once-famous newsman from the east had said that our city was dying, that soon the only people left in Regina would be old or native. For most of us that prospect seemed a lot more comfortable than living in a city filled with once-famous newsmen. I finished my tea and looked at the big clock over the coffee machines. It was ten forty-five.

The waitress came over and asked if I wanted a refill. She was a pretty young woman, with the dark slanted eyes some northern Cree people have. On her uniform was a button saying, "Smile, God Loves You."

I ordered another iced tea. She brought it, then picked up a damp cloth and began wiping down the counter.

"Closing time?" I said.

"I wish," she said.

The outside door opened and two young women came in. You didn't have to be a sociologist or a cop to know how they earned their living. Low-cut sweaters, high-cut skirts, bare legs, shoes with three-inch heels. The smaller of the women was holding her hand against her cheek. Without a word, the waitress scooped up some ice, dropped it in a cloth and handed it to her.

"Thanks, Albertine," the woman holding her face said. Her voice was muffled by her hand.

The other girl said, "Two Diet Cokes. Is it too late for fries?" Albertine shook her head, and the young woman with the swollen face said, "My lucky night. Two fries with gravy."

Then in the same flat voice with which she'd ordered the fries, she said to her companion, "Two blow jobs, two hand jobs and a half and half, so I'm thinking that's enough. It's too fucking hot for anybody to want to get laid, I'm going home, and if Rick says I didn't make my quota, tough. Then this suit pulls up in a Buick and we go to the Ramada, and it's cool there, and I think my fucking luck is maybe changing. A hundred, and all he wants is to do some lines of blow right off my belly, so it looks like an easy evening. Anyway, I'm lying there in the air conditioning with this pig snorting along my stomach, thinking I'll maybe get home in time to watch Letterman, when he goes berserk and starts beating the shit out of me. I got out of there, but the asshole just about caved in my face. Asshole." Then she lapsed into silence.

I got up and walked past them toward the bathroom. The one who had been talking had a pocket mirror in her hand. She was looking at her reflection with anxious eyes as she smoothed pancake makeup over the swelling line of her cheekbone.

When I came back, Albertine was bringing the Cokes and the fries and gravy – Angus's favourite, too. Up close, these girls didn't look much older than Angus, but, as I listened to their young voices trading street stories, I knew that the dates that appeared on their birth certificates were irrelevant. The morning Mieka had found Bernice Morin's body, one of the cops had given Bernice her epitaph. "She was a veteran," he had said. As I watched these girls, carefully eating French fries through lips thick with gloss, laughing at the vagaries of a world that should have been inconceivable, I thought that they were veterans, too.

Kim Barilko never showed up. I waited till midnight, then, bone weary and depressed, I gave up. I was tired of tilting at windmills. When I got home, I went upstairs to shower. After twenty minutes under the hot water, I still didn't feel clean.

The next morning was overcast – more than overcast. The skies were heavy with rain, and the air was ominously still.

When Taylor and I were leaving the house, the first drops began. Angus came out the front door just as we were getting in the car.

"Did you take out the garbage?" I asked.

He started with an excuse.

"No excuses," I said. "You better get it out quick before the rain hits."

Grumbling, he threw his books down on the porch and ran into the house. "You're my hero," I yelled, and Taylor and I drove off.

When I came back fifteen minutes later, it was raining hard. Angus's schoolbooks were still on the front porch. I went into the house, calling his name. Uneasy, I opened the door to the backyard. Angus wasn't there, and the gate that opened into the back alley was open. Angus never left that gate open. He always worried that harm would come to the dogs if they got out of our backyard. As I ran toward the gate, I felt the edge of panic.

There was a puddle just past the gate. I jumped it, but when I came down, I lost my footing in the mud and fell. In a split second, our collie, Sadie, was with me. My husband had always made jokes about Sadie. She was a beautiful animal, but not a smart one. Ian used to call her the show girl. That day the show girl was right on the money. She put her nose under my shoulder and tried to push me up. Then she barked and loped down the alley. She stopped in front of our garbage bin. Our other dog was there, and so was Angus. He was lying in the mud, moaning. I pushed myself up and went to him. His face was ashen.

"The garbage," he said, in a small, strangled voice.

"Don't worry about the garbage," I said. "What happened to you?"

Mute, he shook his head. His eyes were wide with shock. He put his arms around my neck and pulled himself up.

"Don't look in the garbage," he said.

I lifted him up and carried him into the house. He was a dead weight and he was covered in mud. I put him on the chair in the kitchen, and he sat there staring into space, holding his leg and crying. His behaviour scared me. Our kids had had their share of sports injuries, but after the first shock, they'd rallied. Angus wasn't rallying. In fact, he seemed to be sinking deeper into pain.

"I'm taking you to emergency," I said. "I think we should let a doctor have a look at you."

"Don't leave her there," he said. "We can't go to the hospital and just leave her out there."

"Leave who?" I said. "I got the dogs in. We're all okay."

"There's a girl out there in our garbage," he said. "She's dead."

I looked at him. Telling me seemed to calm him. I ran through the yard to the alley. Our city sanitation unit uses industrial waste bins, the kind a garbage truck can unload automatically. I looked into ours. On top of the garbage there was a girl. She was lying on her back. Her peroxided Madonna hair shot out like a halo around the bloody ruins of what had once been her face. Her shirt was soaked with blood, but the rain had washed one patch clean, and I could make out the original colour. Popsicle orange. I would have known it anywhere. Suddenly the air was split with the sound of screaming. Frozen, I listened until somewhere inside, I recognized the voice of the screamer as my own.

The next minutes still have a special terrible clarity for me. I ran to the house. I put on the kettle, called the doctor, and then I called the police. I called Mieka at Judgements, told her there had been a problem at home and asked her to pick Taylor up from school at lunchtime and take her somewhere. I could hear Mieka's voice, urgent, still asking questions, when I hung up the phone. The kettle boiled. I made

Angus tea with a lot of sugar and gave him two Aspirins, then I sat at the kitchen table with him until the police and our doctor came.

The police made it first. I had thought when I met Inspector Tom Zaba that he had the kind of face that was made for smiling, but when I looked at him as he came through the doorway of our kitchen that morning I thought he would never smile again. He was wearing a slicker and he was soaked with rain. Even the ends of his moustache drooped with wet. He looked ineffably sad.

When our doctor came, she took one look at Angus's leg and said he needed to be seen by an orthopedic surgeon. Inspector Zaba asked if he could talk to Angus first. She agreed.

Inspector Zaba was very gentle with Angus, and he was very gentle with me. But all the gentleness in the world couldn't undo the horror of what had happened to Kim Barilko. From my kitchen window I could see police cars driving along the rain-pounded alley, disgorging people into the muddy gravel so they could bag evidence and measure and photograph and turn the last hours of a human life into something that could be contained in a storage box. An RCMP cruiser pulled up, and I saw Constable Perry Kequahtooway get out. Outside the rain pounded on, implacable.

When I'd finished answering Inspector Zaba's questions, I stood up to go to the hospital with Angus.

Inspector Zaba stood, too. "One more question, Mrs. Kilbourn," he said. "Was Kim Barilko on her way to tell you something last night?"

"No," I said, "I was going to tell her something. There was someone I knew who wanted to help Kim make some changes in her life." I told him about the Lily Pad and the mentor program, and he wrote it down without comment.

When he'd finished, he put the cap on his pen and fixed it in his shirt pocket.

"Mrs. Kilbourn, you must have been struck by the pattern here," he said. "Two girls are murdered in less than a month, and a third young woman commits suicide. In all three instances, a member of your family is on the scene when the death is discovered. Bernice Morin dies hours after she is seen by Christy Sinclair. Two days later, Christy Sinclair dies. Kim Barilko goes to Christy Sinclair's funeral, and now she dies. There's got to be a connection."

"I know," I said dully. "I just don't know what it is. But I have to know something. Did Kim have a tattoo? A teddy bear tattoo on her left buttock?"

He looked at me hard, and in his eyes I could see the bleak knowledge of human depravity that had been in Jill Osiowy's eyes when she had shown me the photos of the Little Flower murders.

"No tattoo," he said. "But there was another trademark. Kim Barilko's tongue was split," he said simply. "Someone had slit it right from the tip to the place where it hinged at the back of her mouth."

I could feel the gorge rise in the back of my throat, and I covered my mouth with my hands.

"Why?" I said.

Inspector Tom Zaba was impassive. "The tongue thing is a street punishment for a snitch." He waited for a beat. "I'm not swaggering when I tell you this, Mrs. Kilbourn. I'm trying to impress you with the fact that these people don't have a special code for dealing with nice ladies who want to help fallen girls. If you're in their way, they'll kill you. It's that simple. I don't think either of us wants to see that. Stay away, Mrs. Kilbourn. These people play by rules a woman like you couldn't even begin to understand."

As we pulled up at the emergency ward, Inspector Zaba's warning was replaying itself in my head. Our doctor and the police officer who'd come with us to the hospital took Angus up to X-ray and I sat alone in the emergency room, waiting. I don't know how long I waited. Twice, volunteers, nice-looking women with pastel smocks and expensive perfume, came over to ask if they could get me anything, but I waved them away. My mind had gone into white space. When the orthopedic surgeon came to tell me about the extent of Angus's injury, I had trouble for a minute sorting out what he was talking about. He was an earnest young man with a quick grin and a reassuring manner. His identification tag said his name was Dr. Eric Leung.

"We've X-rayed it twice," he said. "It's a simple triangular break in the tibia." He touched the front of his leg to show me. "Angus tells me when he saw the dead girl, he started running and his toe caught on something and snapped his foot back. There's no need for surgery. You can come back with me while I put the cast on, if you like."

I followed him into the elevator.

"Angus will need the cast for about three weeks," he said. He looked at me. "Are you all right, Mrs. Kilbourn? The break could have been a lot worse. It was really a lucky break." Then, shaking his head at his joke, he stepped out of the elevator.

As I followed him down the hall, the words pounded against my consciousness. Lucky break, lucky break. The boy at the Lily Pad had dropped his guard long enough to say that Kim Barilko needed a lucky break. Now my son had one. Who made the decision about who lost and who won? As I stepped into the brightly lit cast room, I knew I didn't want to know the answer.

When Angus and I went home an hour and a half later, Mieka and Greg were waiting at the front door. Angus was still punchy from the Demerol, so Greg carried him to his bedroom, and Mieka went along to tuck him in.

I was pretty punchy myself. I was trying to decide whether I wanted a cup of tea or three fingers of bourbon when Jill Osiowy walked out of our kitchen. She was ashen, and her eyes were swollen.

"It was the girl I was supposed to be the mentor for, wasn't it?" Jill said.

I nodded.

"One of our guys lives in your neighbourhood. He took some footage of her. I couldn't believe it . . ." Jill's voice was very small and quiet. "I think you have to back off, Jo. They're starting to get close to your family now."

"I think we should both back off," I said.

Jill raked her hands through her hair. "No," she said, "I'm not giving up. If the network won't give me any help on this, I'll do it on my own time. People can't be allowed to get away with this."

I put my arms around her. "No," I said, "they can't. But, Jill, I don't want to think about any of this right now. In fact, for about twenty-four hours I don't want to think about anything."

Just then the phone rang. Jill shook her head. "Good luck with that wish," she said.

It was Peter. He'd just gotten Mieka's message to call. When he heard the news, he said he was coming home. I told him not to. He said he was coming anyway. Then Keith called from Toronto. He said he was coming back on the four o'clock flight. It was going to be a full house.

By seven-thirty everyone was sitting in the living room. Only Taylor and Angus were missing. Samantha's mother had called offering to take Taylor for the night, and Angus had eaten a bowl of Cap'n Crunch and slipped back to sleep.

It was an awkward evening. After the initial embraces and reassurances, no one knew what to do next. The wound of Kim Barilko's death was too fresh for reflection and too overwhelming to make other conversation possible. At nine, the storm knocked the power out, and I think all of us were grateful for the sense of purpose hunting down candles and flashlights gave us. Mieka and Greg took candles to the kitchen and came back a little later with a tray of sandwiches and beer. It was reassuring to know that in a world of unspeakable horror, we could still handle the small stuff.

At eleven, the power came back on, and we watched the local news. Everyone was silent as the image of our house filled the screen. The camera lingered just long enough for the curious to know which house to stop in front of when they came looking, then there was a long shot of our back fence and our cottonwood tree, and finally, the big payoff, our garbage bin. There wasn't much information, just that there had been a murder and mutilation; that the victim, a fifteen-year-old girl, had been found in a garbage bin beside Wascana Creek in South Regina. Name was being withheld until notification, et cetera.

The next story was the storm. There were shots of trees with severed limbs and scarred trunks, of people being rescued from cars trapped in underpasses, and on the lighter side, as the news reporter said, shots of kids waving and grinning as they canoed down residential streets. When the news was over, I turned off the television. In the sudden silence I sat awkwardly twirling the Wandering Soul bracelet on my wrist till Mieka suggested we all go to bed.

The kids went up to shower, and Keith and I were left alone in the kitchen. I walked to the window that faced the backyard. I'd opened it that morning to let the fresh air in. It was still open; in the distance I could hear a radio playing. I stood for a moment, listening, looking at the soft fuzz of yellow the garage lights made in the rainy night. Keith came over and put his arms around me.

"I'm wondering if anything is ever going to be the same again," I said.

He pulled me closer, but he didn't answer.

It rained more that June than it had since our provincial weather bureau began record keeping, but the really bad storms began on the day of Kim Barilko's death. That night as I listened to the rain falling, implacable, unrelenting, images of Kim kept swimming up behind my eyes. Sometimes the image was of her face the day we had walked to the Lily Pad together, defiant behind the makeup mask that couldn't disguise the pubescent bumps of a child's skin. Then, horribly, there was the other face, the appalling mutilation I had seen that morning. Outside the thunder cracked and the lightning split the skies. It would have been comforting to believe the heavens were crying for Kim Barilko. It would have been comforting, but it would have been a crock.

CHAPTER

9

The letter came the last week of June. For three weeks I had made a conscious effort to pull Angus and me back into our old, safe world. The small triangular break in Angus's tibia that I had seen on the X-ray was just the tip of the iceberg. More than one fragile bone had been shattered by the grim reality of Kim Barilko's death, and the knitting together of these hidden fractures was not going to be easy.

Kim Barilko's murder didn't have much staying power as far as the media was concerned. By the time the weekend edition of the newspaper was published, the story had moved off the front page to page five; the following Monday, it had disappeared altogether.

But for me Kim would not disappear. Our last official visit from Inspector Zaba came late Friday afternoon. He had shaved his moustache, and the pale line of his lip made him look more wounded by life than ever. His news wasn't much. Forensic evidence seemed to suggest that Kim had not been killed in our alley. She had been murdered somewhere else and dumped there. There were no leads to the identity of her murderer.

"Trust me, Mrs. Kilbourn, this is not surprising in a street death," he had said. "Most of the time we don't settle these things. The Lily Pad angle was a blank, too. The board of that place is as close to an elite as you'll find in a city this size." He sounded exhausted.

When he left, he warned me again about the need to be careful. "Put this behind you, Mrs. Kilbourn. Put the experience behind you, and put the people behind you. What's done is done."

But try as I might, I could not put Kim Barilko's death behind me because there was no doubt in my mind that I was responsible for it. Keith had tried to reassure me: "Jo, you don't like it and I don't like it, but face facts. The day Kim was born a lot of things were already settled for her, and one of those things was that she wasn't going to live to a ripe old age. You know the kind of world she lived in. Violence is always the first option there. You can't hold yourself responsible for being part of her life when someone exercised that option."

"That's the third time I've heard that argument," I said. "I still don't believe it."

"Believe it," Keith said.

And I tried. I tried, because the alternative was unbearable. In those first days, I was haunted by my guilt. If I had reached out to Christy Sinclair, she wouldn't have committed suicide; if I had left Kim Barilko alone, she wouldn't have been murdered.

Saturday morning, Corporal Perry Kequahtooway came to visit. There had been a break in the weather. It was still overcast, but the rain had stopped. As soon as she got up, Taylor put on her bathing suit and went out to the backyard to run through the pools of standing water with the dogs. I took a towel, dried off the picnic bench and took my coffee outside to watch. When the dogs got tired, they flopped down near the sand pile; Taylor knelt beside them and began building a castle.

Perry Kequahtooway seemed to appear out of nowhere. Suddenly he was there at my elbow. "I rang the doorbell, but I guess you couldn't hear out back."

"I wasn't listening," I said.

He looked concerned. "I wanted to see how you were doing. After the advice I gave you when Christy Sinclair died, I feel responsible."

"Welcome to the club," I said.

He frowned. "Anyway, this is just a personal visit."

For the first time I noticed that he wasn't wearing a uniform. He was dressed in blue jeans and a sweatshirt that said, "Standing Buffalo Powwow, August 9, 10, 11, 1990."

"Can I get you some coffee?" I asked.

"That would be nice," he said.

When I came back, he and Taylor were carrying a bucket of wet gravel from the back alley.

"Is it okay to take that from city property?" I asked.

"It's a very small bucket," he said, "and I think this land used to belong to a relative of mine. You can accept it as a gift from my family to yours." He dumped the gravel carefully at the edge of Taylor's sand pile. "There's more need for it to be here anyway. Your daughter tells me that no matter how carefully she builds her castle, it keeps falling down. It needs a firmer foundation."

"I think I learned a song about that at Sunday school," I said.

He smiled. "Me, too."

Taylor, happy, smoothed the wet gravel into a base for her castle. Perry Kequahtooway and I sipped our coffee.

"I guess you're having a pretty rough time," he said.

"You guess right."

"Blaming yourself?"

"Yeah," I said, "I am. But you know I was only trying to help. I just wanted to help her have a better life."

He was silent. The sun glinted on his dark braids as he looked into the coffee cup between his hands.

"I imagine you've heard that one before," I said.

"Yeah," he said, "I have. It was at the same place where I learned the song about building my house on a firm foundation."

He reached across the table and touched my hand. "That doesn't make it wrong, you know, Mrs. Kilbourn. People have to keep trying. People have to keep trying to do right."

After he left, I tried to hold on to his words. The problem was that everyone seemed to know what was right but me. The family certainly knew. They were with Inspector Zaba. "Leave it alone," they said, and I did my best. I put the Wandering Soul bracelet in a lacquered box where I kept jewellery I didn't wear much any more, and I ignored the pang I felt when I shut the lid. I tried, in the words of the advice columns, to get on with my life. I read and I watched baseball with Angus. I talked to Greg's and Mieka's Saskatoon friends about a surprise party they wanted to hold at our house on the Canada Day weekend. I did all the right things, but I still felt as if someone had kicked me in the stomach.

The Monday morning before the long weekend Jill called and asked me to meet her in the NationTV cafeteria. After I got the kids off to school, I drove over. It was another rainy day. This rain was soft and misting. The Inuit people are said to have twenty-three words for kinds of snow; I thought by the time this spring was over, the people of our city would need at least that many words for kinds of rain. The cafeteria was empty when I arrived. I took my tea over to the window and sat looking at the patio that ran along the building. A man and a woman came out of the building and huddled under the eaves. The man was carrying a yellow slicker, and he draped it around both their shoulders. Lovers, I thought, risking the rain for a moment alone. Then they both pulled out cigarette packs and lit up.

When Jill came, I pointed to the couple. "Driven into each other's arms by the network's no-smoking regulation."

Jill glanced at them, then collapsed into the chair opposite me. "It's been seven years since you and I quit, and I still miss it. Actually, one more phone call from the powers that be, and I may start again."

"If you have a problem and you start smoking again, you have two problems," I said. "That's what they taught us in quit-smoking class, remember?"

Jill narrowed her eyes. "You know, Jo, you can be really obnoxious when you put a little effort into it." She shrugged. "Anyway, what I wanted to talk about was tonight's show. How would you feel about discussing street kids?"

"I thought that was a forbidden subject."

"No, the Little Flower case is a forbidden subject, but I don't see why you can't talk in general terms about these kids."

"As a kind of flesh-and-blood reminder of the rotting infrastructure of our cities?" I said. "That's a quote from the Montreal *Gazette*."

She looked at me approvingly. "Yeah, that's the angle. I'm going to check with Keith and Senator Sam, but if you're game, it sounds like good television to me."

We walked out of the cafeteria together and down to Jill's office. In the hall outside the news division there was a large portrait. Jill stopped in front of it, pulled a black marking pen out of her purse and drew horns on the man in the picture.

"Childish, but it helps," Jill said.

I looked more closely at the man. He looked affluent and assured. He also looked familiar.

"Who is that?" I asked.

Jill looked surprised. "That's my boss. Your boss, too, come to think of it. That's Con O'Malley, the boss of everybody. The head of NationTV."

Jill went into her office. I stayed behind looking at Con O'Malley. He was the man in the photographs I'd seen on Lorraine Harris's desk that morning at the lake, the one reaching out to touch the flame-coloured hibiscus in Lorraine Harris's hair.

It was a small world.

That night, for the first time, our political panel generated as much light as heat. I accused Keith's party of Darwinian social policies; he accused me of believing that you can solve any problem by throwing money at it. Senator Sam Steinitz sat back with a cherubic smile, calculating the number of voters Keith and I were alienating with our intransigence.

When the red light went out, Jill was beaming. "Good show, guys," she said. "I mean that. This is what we should be doing all the time."

Afterwards, Keith walked me home through the park. "You were good tonight," he said. "Sometimes you're a little tentative, but not this time. You really tore a strip off me a couple of times."

"You seemed to handle it all right," I said.

"I've been clawed at by experts, Jo. I still have the wounds."

I slipped my arm around his waist. "Show me," I said.

"Here?" he said.

"Your place might be a little less public."

We went to Keith's. He took the phone off the hook and put on Glenn Gould's final version of the Goldberg Variations. That night when we walked down the hall to Keith's room, I didn't have any doubts. I wanted to have sex with Keith Harris. We undressed quickly and without embarrassment, and when we came together on the bed, our lovemaking was everything lovemaking should be, exciting and tender and fun. Keith was a skilled and considerate partner, and afterwards, as I lay in the dark, I felt relaxed and very happy.

"Jill and I were talking about smoking today," I said. "Right now, I wish I had a cigarette. The one after sex was always the best one."

Keith pushed himself up on his elbow. "I'll run out and get you a pack."

I kissed him. "I don't need cigarettes, I just need a distraction," I said.

"I don't have to be asked twice," he said.

And he didn't.

After I'd dressed, I went to the bureau to brush my hair. Keith was sitting on the bed putting on his shoes; I could see his reflection in the mirror.

"When I was at NationTV this morning, I saw a picture of Con O'Malley," I said. "I didn't realize he and Lorraine were friends."

"They've been friends for years," Keith said, bending to tie a shoelace. "I think probably it's more than that. Lorraine spends a lot of time in Toronto. But she's so cagey about her life, I don't know. To be honest, I was never that interested."

"Do you think she would have asked him to hire me?" I said. "You'll have to admit I'm not exactly a national name like you and Sam."

"You will be," Keith said. "But to answer your question about Lorraine, I'd be very surprised to learn she'd recommended you to Con."

"I guess I'd be surprised, too," I said. "Lorraine never struck me as being the kind of woman who would help another woman along."

Keith came over and stood beside me. "I don't think it's that," he said. "It's just that . . ." His reflection in the mirror smiled sheepishly. "Jo, let's just let this one drop."

"Lorraine doesn't like me, does she?" I said, and I was amazed I hadn't had the insight before.

Keith looked steadily at my reflection.

"Don't worry about hurting my feelings," I said. "I really do want to know. She's going to be Mieka's mother-in-law at the end of the summer. If there's something I'm doing wrong, I should know."

Keith put his hand on my shoulder and turned me so I was facing him.

"It's nothing you're doing. Lorraine just has trouble with women like you."

"Women like me? I don't understand."

"Jo, your father was a doctor. You lived in a big house, you went to a private school, then to university, and after university you married a lawyer. You didn't have to work for things the way Lorraine did. She thinks you've had a pretty easy passage."

I was astounded. "Keith, Lorraine has so much."

"She didn't always have it," Keith said, "and I think that still makes all the difference to her."

When I got home, there was a note from Mieka. Jill had called. Kim Barilko's mother, Angie, was in town to arrange for the burial. I had told Jill I wanted to talk to her. In Mieka's careful backhand was the name of the hotel where Angie Barilko was staying. It was a downtown motor hotel that I knew by reputation called the Golden Sheaf. Most often newspaper stories about it began with the phrase, "The victim was found . . ."

I called Angie Barilko's room. When she answered, her voice was as flat as Kim's. Yes, it was tragic about Kim. Yes, Kim had had so much ahead of her. Yes, I could come over if I wanted to. We agreed to meet in an hour in the Golden Sheaf's coffee shop.

It was in the basement, and it smelled heavily of cigarette smoke and stale beer. The booths were all filled and I sat at the counter. Reflexively, I picked up the menu. The heavy wine leather cover was encased in plastic, and the plastic was sticky.

Angie Barilko had told me she'd be wearing pink; it was an unnecessary identification. I would have known her anywhere. She was Kim twenty years down the line: body bird thin, hair so dead from peroxide and back combing it looked synthetic. She was wearing a hot pink sleeveless blouse, black spandex pants that stopped at mid-calf and three-inch heels. I called her name and she came over and sat on the stool beside me. She lit a cigarette and blew a careful smoke ring in my direction.

"So you knew my girl," she said.

"No," I said, "I didn't, but I wanted to. I thought maybe you could tell me about her."

"You came to the wrong place," she said. "Me and her kind of drifted apart. She was a good kid and all, I don't mean that. It's just nobody ever handed me anything. I've had to work pretty hard just to keep myself going. Rent, food, these . . ." She held up her cigarette pack. "Christ, they really gouge you for these now."

Her first cigarette was burning in the ashtray, but she still opened the pack. "Empty," she said sadly. "Listen, I think I musta left my wallet in the room. Would you happen to have a couple of bucks on you?"

I gave her ten. She came back with cigarettes, but she didn't sit down. Unexpectedly, she smiled.

"Look," she said, "let's be up front. I haven't got a lot to say. Kim mostly stayed at her grandmother's back home."

"Where was home?" I asked.

She was suddenly alert. "You don't want to know that," she said. Then she smiled slyly. "Look, I don't want you going away mad, feeling like I didn't keep up my end of the bargain. Here's a picture of her."

She pulled out her wallet. Her subterfuge revealed, she opened her eyes in mock surprise. "Shit, it was here all along. Anyway, here she is."

In the picture, Kim was perhaps three: blonde, ponytailed, sweet. She was sitting on a man's knee and holding a beer up to his lips.

"She was a cutie, eh?" Angie said. And then to herself, not me, she said, "I wish I could remember the name of that guy." She shrugged. "Water under the bridge. Anyways, I'm taking her back to Calgary to bury. We got nobody here any more."

I went home feeling overwhelmed with sadness, but with a sense that perhaps something was ended. The week after Angie Barilko took her daughter home it seemed possible to believe that the brutal blows that had begun the morning Mieka discovered Bernice Morin's body had stopped. Lorraine and I had some nice moments together planning and shopping. She was an extraordinarily competent woman, and as I watched her tick off the tasks in Greg's and Mieka's wedding plans book, I was filled with admiration. I told her a couple of stories about my childhood that put it in a less enviable light, and I could feel her warm to me. Mieka took to calling us "the mothers," and the night Lorraine and I addressed the wedding invitations, Mieka snapped a whole roll of film of us. "For the grandchildren," she said, and Lorraine and I looked at one another and smiled.

Life seemed to be looking up for Peter, too. One night he called, sounding even less forthcoming than usual, but after a few false starts, he told me he had met a young woman. A horse trainer.

"Marriage made in heaven," Mieka said, rolling her eyes when I told her. "They can currycomb each other."

Taylor began her sketching classes. I bought her a Sunday *New York Times* that had a review of a retrospective of her mother's work, and she carried it everywhere with her for three days, then she asked for some oils so she could get started making real art.

Angus became agile with his crutches. One night when the rain stopped long enough for the league to schedule a ball game for his team, he sat in the bleachers and cheered. Then when the game was over, he ran the bases on his walking cast, laughing like a maniac all the way.

On the last morning in June I drove him down to the hospital and the orthopedic surgeon removed the cast. Unconsciously, I had established a one-to-one relationship between the healing of Angus's leg and the healing of our lives. As the cast came away and that pale, barely mended leg came into view, the symbolism was pretty breathtaking.

When we got back from the hospital, Jill Osiowy was standing at the front door. She was wearing shorts and an outsized T-shirt with the logo of *Frank* magazine on the front. Angus had brought his cast home from the hospital. It was an eerie trophy; it looked like an amputation, but Jill was enthusiastic as she examined it. Then Taylor grabbed Jill's hand and took her into the backyard to show off her bean patch. I followed along, and when Jill had finished enthusing about the beans, I said, "My turn now. I haven't got anything to show off, but I've got beer."

"You win," Jill said. "Anyway, I came because I have something for you." She handed me a letter. "Fan mail," she said. "I'll get the beer. Read your letter."

It had been opened and stamped with the network's name and the date of receipt. The notepaper was commercial, from a motel called the Northern Lights, Box 720, Havre Lake, Saskatchewan. The writing was carefully rounded, and the writer had used a liner. It looked like the work of a conscientious grade seven student, but it wasn't.

> Dear Mrs. Kilbourn,
>
> I've written this letter twenty times and torn it up. My husband says what's passed is passed, and usually he is right, but sometimes it seems Fate takes a hand. I wouldn't usually watch a show about Politics. Politics is not for me, (no offence), but I was interested in your topic June 3 when you talked about Street Kids. I recognized you right away. You are the woman who was like a mother to Theresa Desjarlais. When I saw in the paper that Theresa had passed away I thought of you but I had forgotten your name till I saw you that night. It is you. The picture Theresa brought me of the two of you at Christmas was framed. It is on top of our TV, so there's no mistake.
>
> I know you must be very busy, but Theresa was my friend and I want to know if she was happy before she passed away.
>
> This matters to me.
>
> Sincerely
> Mrs. Tom Mirasty (Beth)

Jill came back with the beer.

"I've read it, of course. Some of the mail we get isn't worth handing along."

I looked at her. "Did you notice the address? Havre Lake. I'm going to be driving right past there this weekend when I take Angus to camp."

Jill sipped her beer. "I thought you'd decided that discretion was the better part of valour. I notice you're not wearing the bracelet any more."

"Maybe it's time I put it back on," I said.

For a long time neither of us said anything. We sat and watched Taylor in her sand pile, building her elaborate city. In the days since Perry Kequahtooway visited, the castle had become a wondrous thing. When there wasn't room for one more cupola or turret, Taylor had sculpted a wall, high and protective. What was inside was worth protecting. On the grounds of her castle Taylor had created a beautiful world of looking-glass lakes and pebble staircases and tiny forests made out of cedar cuttings. When I was a child, I had dreamed of living in a place like that: a castle with a population of one where nothing could ever hurt me and no one could ever make me do things I didn't want to do. But I wasn't a child any more.

I looked at Beth Mirasty's letter. "This matters to me," she had written; I knew it mattered to me, too.

I turned to Jill. "I'm going to see her," I said. "I'm going to see Beth Mirasty. She's right. Sometimes it seems as if fate does take a hand."

Jill's brow furrowed. "Just be sure it's fate in there directing things," she said. "I've got a feeling about this one. Don't take things at face value here. For once in your life, Jo, don't assume the best."

"I'll be careful," I promised. "And you can warn me again when we tape the Canada Day show. 'A Time for Patriotism not Cynicism,' right?"

She shuddered. "Does that topic make you want to throw up, too? Anyway, taping ahead will give everybody the long weekend off, and nobody will be watching, anyway."

"Good," I said. "I'll wear that flowered dress I wore the first night. Get my money's worth."

That afternoon I drove to the liquor store to pick up the wine for Greg's and Mieka's surprise party. I was just about to pull out of the parking lot when Helmut Keating came out of the side door of the liquor store. He was close enough for me to see that he was wearing his "Let Me Be Part of Your Dream" sweatshirt, but he didn't see me. He was too busy supervising the employee who was pushing the dolly with his order on it. I watched as the two men unloaded the cases of liquor into a Jeep Cherokee, and when they went back inside, I waited. Five minutes later they came out with another load. They made four trips in all.

When Helmut pulled out of the parking lot, the only part of the Cherokee that wasn't loaded with liquor was the front seat. Whatever dream Helmut was going to be a part of was going to be a festive one. He drove north on Albert Street, turned off at the first side street past the Lily Pad, then doubled back. He pulled the Cherokee close to the back door of the Lily Pad and unloaded the liquor himself. That didn't make sense. There had been a half-dozen kids lying on the grass by the plywood frog on the front lawn, and Helmut wasn't the kind of guy who would feel he had to spare them on a hot day.

It took him half an hour to unload the liquor. When he came out of the Lily Pad for the last time he looked hot and unhappy. He got into the Cherokee and roared out of the parking lot. As he drove off, I noticed his licence plate: "ICARE," it said. I cared, too. I walked to the back door. It looked as if it had been designed to withstand a nuclear attack. The lock was the kind that was activated by a card; there was a sticker next to it that said, "SLC Security Systems." High-powered stuff for the back door of a drop-in centre for street kids.

I looked up at the old three-storey house that had been converted into the Lily Pad. There was nothing welcoming about the building from the back. There were no windows at ground level, and the windows on the upper storeys were closed off with blinds. It didn't look like a place that would give up answers easily.

The sun glinted off my Wandering Soul bracelet. I remembered Kim Barilko saying that she had known Christy Sinclair "from home and then at the Lily Pad. She was going to be my mentor." Now Kim was dead and Christy was dead.

I began to trace the incised letters on the bracelet with my fingertip. "Wandering Soul Pray For Me." "What's happening here, Christy?" I said. "What's going on?" A cat leaped from nowhere and landed at my feet with a feral scream. I ran to the car and slammed the door behind me. It was broad daylight in the city where I'd lived most of my adult life, but my heart was pounding as if I were approaching the heart of darkness.

"You're being crazy," I said, "overreacting." I locked the car doors and took deep breaths until I was calm enough to turn the key in the ignition. As I drove south along Albert Street, I tried to comfort myself with the familiar. I knew the buildings and trees on that street as intimately as I knew the back of my hand. "You're almost home," I said. "You're safe." But as I pulled into the alley behind my house, I was still shaking violently. My body knew what my mind wouldn't admit. The darkness I had felt at the Lily Pad wasn't something I could lock my doors against or drive away from. It was all around me.

Saturday night was Greg's and Mieka's surprise party. I had two jobs: to leave a key in the mailbox and to get the guests of honour out of the way. Keith offered to take us all for an early dinner at a restaurant about fifteen miles from the city. The place was called Stella's. The decor was 1950s, the music was jukebox, and the food was very good. Everything went off without a hitch.

I'd given Lorraine a key so she could welcome guests, and when we opened the front door, Mieka and Greg were met by a room filled with exuberant friends. It was a great party. Despite the fact that their wedding was two months away, Mieka and Greg were genuinely shocked – events of the past weeks had, I think, undermined their belief in happy surprises. But their friends had pulled it off, and their success made these handsome young men and women more ebullient than ever. Taylor was in her element. She loved excitement and colour and looking at people. Angus had fun, too. He was on the cusp of adolescence, sometimes a boy and sometimes a young man. That night as he helped with food and music and talked about Rocket Ismail and the Argonauts, he was a young man, and a happy one.

Lorraine was enjoying herself, too. In fact, she was so relaxed that when we found ourselves alone late in the evening, I decided to ask her if she'd been involved in getting the job for me at NationTV. Before I was even finished the question, I knew I'd made a mistake. Lorraine's smile didn't fade, but her body tensed and her grey eyes grew wary.

I tried to defuse the situation. "I'm only asking because I'm enjoying doing the show so much, and if you smoothed the way for me with Con O'Malley, I wanted to thank you."

Her manner changed. She became almost stagily coquettish. "Jo, I can't imagine how you found out about Con and me, but since you have, I'll tell you this. Our relationship has nothing to do with business. He's my gentleman friend. We have much more exciting things to talk about than NationTV when we're together. I think it's wonderful that they hired you, but the idea didn't come from me." Suddenly, her eyes were wide. "I'm not the only member of the Harris family who's friends with Con O'Malley, you know. Blaine and Keith have known him for years." She stood up and smoothed the skirt of her white linen dress. "Now, if you'll excuse me, I think I'd like to freshen my drink."

After Lorraine left, I was edgy. Her behaviour had been odd. Mieka had said once that Lorraine thought of herself as a "man's woman." If that was the role she'd been playing for me, I hadn't liked it. I poured myself a drink, but it didn't help. Since the night of their engagement party, too much had gone wrong for Greg and Mieka. They deserved a joyous, uncomplicated evening, and I was tense with the fear that my encounter with Lorraine meant they wouldn't get one. For the rest of the evening Lorraine kept her distance from me, but she held her cheek out for a kiss at the front door when she left. As I watched her walk down our front path, her hair silvery in the moonlight, I breathed a sigh of relief. From beginning to end, the evening had been flawless. I was asleep before my head hit the pillow.

In the middle of the night I was awakened by the sound of a woman crying out. I lay there in the dark, heart pounding, hoping the cry had been part of a dream. But as I listened the sound came again. It was outdoors, in the backyard. I jumped out of bed and ran to the window.

Greg and Mieka were in the pool, swimming in the moonlight. The sounds I had heard were the little shrieks Mieka made as Greg dived under her and pulled her toward him in the water. They were naked – skinny-dipping, we used to call it. I could see the pale shapes of their bodies in the dark water. I turned away and then I heard my daughter's voice. "Hey, watch this," she said. I looked out the window.

Mieka was swimming across the pool. Suddenly she disappeared under the water, then in a heartbeat, she stuck her bum up. I could see it gleaming whitely in the moonlight. Greg swam toward her and kissed the smooth white curve. Then he disappeared under the water, too. I waited till they were both above the water, safe, happy, in love. Then I turned and went back to bed. As I lay between the cool sheets, listening to the sounds of the innocent summer night, I was smiling.

Good times. There were good times ahead.

The kids and I went to the early church service the next day, and we spent the rest of the morning getting ready for our trip up north. We were all looking forward to it. Angus and Taylor had been counting the days, and now that life seemed to have smoothed out for the big kids, I was looking forward to a holiday with Keith. We hadn't exactly enjoyed smooth sailing since we met. Jill had arranged for us to do the July eighth show from the network's northern studio, about an hour's drive from where we would be staying. That meant Keith and Taylor and I were going to have ten days of sun and sand and the smell of pines.

Sunday afternoon, I met Keith at the TV studio, and we taped the Canada Day program. It went well, and the minute the technician came and took off our microphones, Keith turned to me.

"Let's go home," he said. I couldn't wait.

When we came out of the studio, the sun was shining. For the first time in a month there wasn't a cloud in sight.

"Look," I said. "Blue skies as far as the eye can see. How's that for an omen?"

Keith stopped in the middle of the sidewalk and took my hand.

"The rain is over and gone," he said. "The flowers appear on the earth; the time of the singing of birds is come, and the voice of the turtle is heard in our land. The fig tree putteth forth her green figs, and the vines with the tender grape give a good smell. Arise, my love, my fair one, and come away."

I put my arms around his neck and drew him toward me. "I wish you'd waited till we were closer to your place before you said that."

"I thought it might make you move a little faster," he murmured.

It did.

As we walked into the apartment, the phone was ringing. Keith made a face. "Should I answer it?"

I shrugged.

He crossed his fingers and picked up the receiver. I knew at once it wasn't good news. He listened for a while, then he said, "I'll be right down."

When he turned to me, his face was serious. "That was Lorraine. She wants me to come downstairs. She's decided it's time to put Blaine in a place where he can get special care."

"Did something happen?" I said.

"Nothing dramatic. I have a feeling Lorraine just took a hard look at the problem and decided to throw in the towel."

"I thought your father was doing better," I said. "Didn't you tell me that he'd put a couple of words together this week?"

"Yeah, but that was the only good news. And there's a lot of bad news. Blaine's getting just about impossible to control. Sean says as soon as he turns around, Blaine tries to get to the telephone or out the door. And he has these rages when Sean brings him back. He's terrible with Lorraine, too. Remember how he was with you that night at the lake? He's like that with her now. It's awful for Lorraine, and of course it could be fatal for my father. Sean worries that Blaine is going to get his blood pressure sky-high and have another stroke." For a moment, he stood silent, lost in thought, then he shook himself.

"Anyway, I'd better get down there. Jo, why don't you fix yourself a drink. I'll be back as soon as I can manage."

When Keith returned, he looked grim.

"So what's going to happen?" I asked.

Keith took my hands in his. "I'm not going to beat around

the bush, Jo. I can't go with you tomorrow. I'm sorrier than I can say, but this just has to be taken care of."

I pulled him close. "Damn," I said. "I was really looking forward to being with you. But I know it can't be helped. You're doing the right thing. Right now, if I could figure out a way to make you do the wrong thing, I would, but that'll pass. I know it isn't all polka dots and moonbeams at our age."

Keith poured us drinks and we took them to the balcony. Across the street in the park, some boys were playing touch football: shirts and skins. The sun was hot; the skins team would be in agony by the end of the day. Toward the lake, a crew was putting up a sound system in the bandshell for Canada Day. I thought how nice it would be to sit with Keith on a blanket in the grass, eating hot dogs and listening to the symphony.

But it wasn't going to be that kind of weekend.

I turned to Keith. "What happens next?" I asked.

He shook his head. "As usual, Lorraine has us organized. She's found a place in Minnesota that's supposed to be terrific. Out in the country, good staff-patient ratio, first-rate special care, and reliable security."

"Security?" I said, surprised.

"I told you that Blaine keeps trying to wander off."

I thought of that proud, elegant old man, and my heart sank. "What an awful thing for him," I said.

Keith looked grim. "I know. That's why Lorraine wants me to fly to Minneapolis with him."

"How soon?" I said.

"Tomorrow," he said.

"Don't you usually have to wait months for places like that?" I said.

For the first time since he'd come upstairs, Keith smiled. "People who aren't Lorraine have to wait months," he said. "But Lorraine always manages to move right to the head of the line. Anyway, this time, let's be glad she was able to pull some strings. If this place is the best thing for Blaine, then it's a case of the sooner the better." He reached over and touched my hair. "Once I get Blaine in, I can come home. If we're lucky, you and I can salvage at least part of our holiday."

"Let's hope we're lucky," I said. "Let's hope."

That night, as I sat at the kitchen table planning the route the kids and I would take to Havre Lake, hope had already given way to stoic acceptance. I'd replaced my new night-gown, silky and seductive, with the flannelette granny gown my neighbour had given me the year Angus was born. I knew that it got cold in the north when you were sleeping alone. There didn't seem to be much to look forward to except a good night's sleep and a seven-hour drive with two kids in the back seat.

Suddenly I thought of my old friend Hilda McCourt. Saskatoon wasn't far out of our way, and I was in need of a sympathetic ear. When I called her, she said she'd be delighted to have us all come for lunch. "A Canada Day menu," she said.

"Beaver soup?" I said.

"If all else fails," she said dryly. "I can assure you that one thing we will have is a bottle of single-malt Scotch. I'm looking forward to toasting our country's birthday with you, Joanne. Now, I'll let you go. You must have preparations. Drive safely. I'll look for you at twelve."

Just the sound of Hilda's voice made me feel better.

By the time I opened the windows, pulled up the blankets and turned out the lights, I was looking forward to the next day. I loved the north, and it would be fun to explore it with the kids. If all went well in Minnesota, Keith would join me, and before the end of the week, the singing of birds and the voice of the turtle would be heard in our land.

The telephone began to ring not long after I fell asleep. My danger sensors must have been off full alert, because I reached for the receiver without a second thought. The sounds I heard were barely human: angry cries and shapeless vowels. Then, very clearly, I heard the familiar word, "Killdeer," and, after a beat, two new words. "The rain," said Blaine Harris in his unused, angry voice. "The rain." Then the line went dead.

As I lay there in the dark listening to the dial tone, I was glad I was getting out of town.

CHAPTER

10

When I woke up on Canada Day the rain had started again. I turned on the radio and lay in bed, listening. The local news was a litany of cancellations: sports days, slow-pitch tournaments, Olde Tyme picnics, tractor pulls, walking tours, bed races, mud flings, parades. Everything was cancelled because of the weather. I remembered Blaine Harris's phone call the night before. "The rain," he'd said. Maybe he'd just been giving me the weather forecast.

I put on my sweats and took the dogs for a run. Greg and Mieka would take care of them while I was away. Somehow, with wedding plans and love in the air, I had the sense that the daily runs might be sporadic. We made an extra-long run: around the lake and home. It was a distance the dogs and I used to do often when we were younger, but it had been a while. By the time we got back, we were all panting and pleased with ourselves.

I fed the dogs, made coffee, showered and spent ten minutes rubbing my body with the expensive lotion Mieka had given me the Christmas before. Finally, wearing the blue dress I had worn the first night I had dinner with Keith,

I slid the bracelet on my wrist. When I felt the bracelet warm against my skin, I understood why I had called Hilda the night before. I had thought then that I needed a sympathetic ear, but that wasn't it. What I needed was advice. Every part of me that answered to the rules of logic said I should let Christy and Kim rest in peace. But life was not always ruled by logic, and Hilda McCourt was a woman who understood this. She would understand the power of the bracelet and the pull of my commitment to those dead girls. Hilda would be my final arbiter. If she thought I was wrong to keep pushing to discover the route by which Theresa Desjarlais had become Christy Sinclair, I'd give up. When I drove north, I'd stop at the Northern Lights Motel, have coffee with Beth Mirasty and tell her that her husband was right: the past was past.

When I came down, Taylor and Angus were sitting at the breakfast table, dressed, with their hair neatly combed, eating Eggos and fresh strawberries. The night before, when I had told Angus that Keith wouldn't be part of our holiday, he had started with his usual barrage of questions, but something in my face must have stopped him. He'd given me a hug and wandered off to bed. He was learning discretion, growing up.

As I looked at Taylor wearing a shirt that was right-side out and socks that matched, it was obvious that Angus had talked to her, too. The exemplary behaviour continued as we ran back and forth to the car, packing in the rain. There were no complaints from anybody about getting wet or about having to leave things behind. We hit the road early, just as the nine o'clock news came on the car radio, and no one suggested we stop for drinks or a bathroom until we drove into Chamberlain, about ninety kilometres from home. The station where we stopped gave out small Canadian flags with a gas purchase. Angus stuck his in his hat and Taylor put hers in her ponytail. They looked so patriotic that the

gas station attendant gave them each a colouring book about
a beaver who wanted to find the true meaning of Canada.
Taylor was usually contemptuous of colouring books, but
the beaver and his friends were cleverly drawn, and as we
pulled away, she was already tracing the lines with her
fingers, making them part of her muscle memory. The rest
of the drive in the rain was quiet and companionable, and I
enjoyed it.

We pulled up in front of Hilda's neat bungalow on Melrose
Avenue just before noon. The Canadian flag was flying from
the porch at the front of Hilda's house, a bright splash of red
and white through the grey mist of rain. As Hilda opened the
door and held her arms out in greeting, there was another
burst of radiant colour. In her early eighties, Hilda McCourt
was still a riveting figure. Today, she was wearing a jumpsuit the colour of a Flanders poppy and her hair, dyed an
even more brilliant red than usual, was swept back by a red-
and-white striped silk scarf.

The kids made a run for the house. Hilda stopped them at
the door. "Let me have a look at you before you disappear,"
she said. She examined them carefully. "Well, you're obviously thriving. There's a jigsaw puzzle on the kitchen table
for you. Quite a challenging one, at least for me. Harold
Town's *Tower of Babble*. Taylor, your mother told me once
that she thought Harold Town was splendid. Why don't you
and Angus have a look and see what you think?"

As we watched the kids run down the hall, Hilda put her
arm through mine. "Now, how about a little Glenfiddich to
ease the traveller?"

I followed her gratefully. As we walked through to the
glassed-in porch at the back of her house, I caught sight of
the table set for lunch in the dining room. Red napkins carefully arranged in crystal water glasses, a white organdy table-
cloth, red zinnias in a creamy earthenware pitcher.

"Lovely," I said.

"Not subtle," she said, "but I don't believe this is the year to be subtle about our country."

Hilda's back room was as individual and fine as she was. On the inside wall, there was an old horsehair chaise longue covered by a lacy afghan. At the foot of the chaise longue was a TV; at the head was a table with a good reading lamp and a stack of magazines. The current issue of *Canadian Forum* was on top. Along the wall, a trestle table held blooming plants. In the centre of the table a space had been cleared for three framed photographs: Robert Stanfield, T.C. Douglas and Pierre Trudeau.

"That's quite a triptych," I said, looking down at them.

"Two men who should have been prime minister and one who probably shouldn't have," Hilda said briskly. Then she tapped the frame of the Trudeau photo. "But what style that man had, and what fun he was."

She poured the Glenfiddich, handed me a glass and raised her own.

"To Canada," she said.

"To Canada," I said.

"Now," she said, "let's sit and watch the rain and you can tell me what brought you here."

As I felt the Scotch warming my body, I realized how much I wanted to talk.

I took off the bracelet and handed it to her. "It all began with this," I said.

She turned it carefully. "'Wandering Soul Pray For Me,'" she said. "Intriguing, but I've seen a bracelet like this before, you know. In fact, there were several of them at the duty-free shop in Belfast. The story was that monks hammered the silver by hand. Whoever did the hammering, these bracelets are costly – in more ways than one, but I presume by your face you've already discovered that. The intent, of course, is to remind the traveller that no matter how far afield she goes, the one left behind is still linked to her." She handed the bracelet back to me. "Who have you left behind, Joanne?"

In the garden a tiny pine siskin was feeding at Hilda's bird feeder. I watched until it flew away, then I turned to Hilda.

"Nobody," I said. "And that's the problem. There are two people I can't seem to leave behind no matter how hard I try."

"And you've decided to confide in me about it."

"I've decided to let you tell me what to do next," I said.

I told her everything, starting with the morning Mieka found Bernice Morin's body in the garbage can behind Judgements and ending with Beth Mirasty's letter.

When I was finished, Hilda looked at me levelly. "And your intention is to go to Havre Lake in search of Christy Sinclair?"

"I don't know," I said. "When I put it all together like this, my behaviour seems quixotic even to me. My husband used to say that there was nothing more terrifying than blind goodness loosed upon the world. You meet a lot of Don Quixotes in politics, you know. Certain they know what's best for everyone, tilting at windmills, rescuing the downtrodden whether they want to be rescued or not. I don't want to be like that, Hilda."

"And yet you can't walk away," she said.

"No," I said. "I can't walk away." I held up the bracelet. "Because of this. Because a woman gave me this bracelet and then she died. And suddenly it wasn't just a bracelet any more. Hilda, tell me honestly. Did you feel the power in this?"

"No," she said, thoughtfully, "but that doesn't mean it's not there. Your grandmother wouldn't have had any trouble putting a name to the pull you're feeling. She would have called it conscience. And she wouldn't have thought you were quixotic. She would have thought you were trying to right a wrong you did to another human being. Joanne, I've been listening carefully to you, and I know why you're so resolute about Christy Sinclair. To use a word that makes people uneasy these days, you feel that you sinned against her. A sin of omission. In your dealings with her you showed a want of *charitas*. Most often that word is translated as charity, but you have Latin, Joanne, you know the correct translation."

"Love," I said. "*Charitas* means love. Christy needed my love and I didn't give it to her." Suddenly, I was tired of the burden. I slammed the bracelet down on the table.

"Damn it, Hilda, how could I love her? She was so unlovable – the lies, the obsessions, the need. She needed so much. Every time I turned around, she was there, needing me to love her." My voice was shrill with exasperation. "How could I love her? I didn't even like her."

"According to Reinhold Niebuhr, God told us to love our enemies, not to like them," Hilda said dryly.

"Reinhold Niebuhr never knew Christy," I said.

The bracelet lay on the table in front of me, a dull circle of reproach. I picked it up and slid it on my wrist.

"It's too late, Hilda," I said. "There's nothing I can do to make it up to her now."

"It's never too late, Joanne. You know that."

"But what do I do?"

Hilda touched my hand. "You know the answer to that as well as I. You ask forgiveness, and then you try to make amends."

She held up the Glenfiddich. "Now before you begin that arduous work, would you like what the Scots call 'a drap for your soul'?"

I held out my glass. "I think my soul could use it," I said.

Lunch was good. Meat loaf, mashed potatoes, garden peas, new carrots, and, for dessert, strawberry Jell-O and real whipped cream. By the time we'd eaten and I'd rounded up the kids, the rain had stopped, and I felt ready for the drive north. Hilda walked with me to the car. We said our good-byes, then she put her hand on my arm.

"I almost forgot to tell you how splendidly you're doing on *Canada Today*. You were a little shaky at the beginning, but now you seem very assured."

"I'm feeling better about it," I said. "And Keith and Sam have been a real help."

"There seems to be a certain warmth between you and Keith Harris."

I could feel myself blush. "Is it that obvious?"

"Only to someone who knows you well," she said. "Is it serious?"

"I don't know," I said. "We've had so many outside problems to deal with. Keith was supposed to be with me today, but his father's condition is worse, so he stayed behind to take care of things."

Hilda's eyes were sad. "I'm sorry to hear that about Blaine."

"You know him?" I said, surprised. "I can't imagine you two travelling in the same circles."

"He was a great proponent of regional libraries, as, of course, am I. We were on any number of boards and committees together when the libraries were being set up."

"What was he like?" I asked. "I didn't meet him until after he'd had his stroke."

Hilda looked thoughtful. "I think Blaine Harris is the most moral man I've ever met. There's an incident I remember particularly. During the summer of 1958, we had a series of community meetings, and after one of them we had lunch at a diner in Whitewood. Later that afternoon we stopped for gas and Blaine noticed he'd received a dollar extra in change from the cashier at the diner. He drove back to Whitewood to return the money. He apologized to me for what he called our thirty-mile detour, but he said he couldn't have slept that night if he hadn't known things were set right. That's the kind of man he was, utterly fair and just."

We spent the night in Prince Albert, a small city 150 kilometres north of Saskatoon, famous for the fact that when it had the choice of being home to the province's university or a federal penitentiary, it chose the pen. In fact, the reason we were stopping in Prince Albert was the jail. Angus had seen a TV program about the prison museum, so late on the afternoon of July 1, Taylor and I were following Angus through dim rooms filled with painfully crafted weapons confiscated from hidden places in the bodies of prisoners. A celebration of Canadian ingenuity.

That night we ate dinner at a Chinese restaurant Ian and I had liked when we had campaigned in the north. Taylor ate a whole order of almond prawns and nodded off at the dinner table. We went to the motel and I switched on *Canada Today*. The warmth between Keith and me was apparent even on TV; just to see him made me lonely for him. I'd forgotten how painful physical longing could be, and after five minutes I turned the television off and took a shower.

We were all in bed by nine o'clock. The kids slipped into sleep easily. I lay in the dark, listening to the radio. There had been a contest earlier that day; people from all over Canada had been asked to call in with their renditions of our national anthem. A physics class from Halifax played ten pop bottles filled with water; four high-school principals from Saskatoon sang a barbershop harmony; a young girl from Manitoba sang in Ojibway; a Canada goose from Don Mills, Ontario, was disqualified because she was a fraud; a Vancouver group called the Raging Grannies offered a social commentary.

O Canada.

I slept well and woke up to a room filled with sunshine and fresh northern air. On impulse I called Peter. The phone rang and rang, and I was about to hang up when Peter answered, sounding breathless and happy. He had just come in – it was a beautiful morning in the southwest, hot already, and still, and he and Susan, the young woman who trained horses, had just come in from riding through the hills.

"It sounds idyllic," I said.

"It is idyllic, Mum," he said quietly. "Everything is starting to look very good again."

"And Susan is . . ."

"Susan is the best part," he said.

"Good," I said. "I love you, Peter."

"Same here, Mum."

I was hanging up when I heard his voice. "Mum, I haven't forgotten Christy."

"Neither have I," I said. Then I did hang up.

The Northern Lights Motel was just off the Hansen Lake Road. It was the kind of place I would have picked to stay in myself: a low-slung log building that housed a restaurant and a store. In the pines out back, I could see a dozen or so log cabins. On each side of the door to the restaurant, truck tires, painted white, bloomed with pink petunias. The effect was clean and cheerful. Other people must have liked the place, too; a no-vacancy sign hung on the hitching post near the entrance.

There were two people in the restaurant. A man, dressed in the newest and best from the Tilley catalogue, sat at a back booth, looking at the menu through round-lensed tortoiseshell glasses. A slender young native woman, wearing blue jeans and a dazzlingly white sleeveless cotton blouse, stood beside him, taking his order. She was a striking figure; her profile was delicate, and her hair, held back from her face by beadwork barrettes, fell shining and straight to her waist.

The kids and I sat down at the counter. There wasn't much of a demarcation between the restaurant and the store. I knew that if I ordered lake trout, the fish would have been swimming in Havre Lake twenty-four hours earlier, but if I ordered beans, the cook would walk three steps to the store and take the beans off the shelf. The wall behind the counter was filled with Polaroids of weekend fishermen squinting into the sun, holding up their prize catches: northern pike, walleye, lake trout, whitefish.

Angus grabbed my arm and pointed to a sign over the cash register: "Shower Free with Meal. Otherwise $3.50. $5.00 deposit on towels."

"That wouldn't exactly bankrupt you, would it?" I whispered.

He grinned, slid off the stool and went over to look at a display of hooks and lures. Taylor followed him.

The woman who had been taking the order came over to our table. She touched my wrist with her index finger.

"Her bracelet," she said softly. "I'm so glad you came, Mrs. Kilbourn. Just let me put in that man's order and we can talk." She turned to Angus. "If you walk down that road out there toward the lake, you'll see my son fishing on the dock. He says the jack are really biting today."

Angus shot me a pleading look.

"Half an hour," I said. "We have to get you settled in camp and get ourselves to Blue Heron Point."

He was out the door in a flash. When Beth Mirasty came back, she had a tray with a pitcher of lemonade and four glasses.

"Let's go out back where we can be quiet," she said. She smiled at Taylor. "Would you like to learn how to make wishbone dolls?" she asked softly. "My kokom's sewing today. She could teach you."

Taylor looked at her curiously. "Is Kokom your little girl?" she asked.

"Kokom is Mrs. Mirasty's grandmother," I said. "That's how you say grandmother in Cree."

The back room appeared to be the family living room. It was simply furnished, and everything in it shone. The linoleum was hard-polished and the pine furniture gleamed. I thought I would like to stay in a motel owned by Beth Mirasty. An old woman sat in a rocking chair by the window. There was a lace curtain behind her, as dazzlingly white as Beth Mirasty's blouse; the old woman was wearing a pink dress, and her white hair was carefully fixed with beadwork combs, pink and green and white. In front of her was a birch basket filled with scraps of fabric. She was sewing one of them onto a quilt on her knee.

When she heard us, the old lady looked up. She didn't smile, but there was something about her that was welcoming.

"The little one would like to know how to make wishbone dolls, Kokom," Beth said.

The old woman leaned forward and said something to Taylor. Then she pointed toward a doorway that seemed to lead into the rest of the flat. Taylor ran off where she had pointed.

"First, you need chicken bones," the old lady said to me.

After Beth introduced us and poured the lemonade, the old lady sat with her hands folded until Taylor came back with a coffee can. The old lady reached into the coffee can, took out a wishbone and handed it to Taylor. "Think about the face you want to put on the little part that sticks out at the top," she said.

In the corner was the TV. A large coloured photo of Christy and me was in a frame on top of it. I went to look closer. It was a shot of us in front of the Christmas tree. Christy was wearing a Santa Claus sweatshirt and red overalls. She was holding an old plastic angel.

I remembered the moment. We were decorating the tree, and after the picture was taken, Christy had asked me to tell her the story of how we got the angel.

I had laughed and said, "Oh, it's just one of those boring family stories."

"Tell me," she said, "please."

And so I had told her how, when Mieka was in kindergarten, she had told her teacher that we were a Catholic family who had lost our angel, and the woman had given it to her for Christmas. And I had told her about how Angus had eaten the pasta off the jar-ring-framed picture of the dogs he had made in grade one, and about the time when Sadie was a pup and Peter had hung dog biscuits on the branches of the tree and we had come down Christmas morning to discover that Sadie had knocked down the tree and eaten the dog biscuits and half the ornaments. Ordinary family stories, but Christy's yearning as I told them had been almost palpable.

Behind me, Beth Mirasty said, "She brought me that picture herself when she came home before New Year's. She was so proud of it."

The week between Christmas and New Year's. We had all planned to go skiing that week. Then, out of nowhere, Christy had announced she was going to Minneapolis with friends. When she came back, she had talked endlessly about the operas they had seen and the restaurants where they had eaten. More lies.

"She said last Christmas was the best one she'd ever had," Beth Mirasty said softly. She picked up the picture and we walked over and sat on a couch in the corner. "Theresa told me you had made her part of your family."

"What about her own family?" I asked.

Beth Mirasty seemed confused. "I thought she'd told you all that."

"No," I said, "she didn't."

Beth looked at the photo. For a long time she didn't say anything, and I had the sense that she was deciding whether to go on. Finally, she shook her head.

"I guess it doesn't matter any more," she said. "They're all passed away except Jackie. He's Theresa's brother, and he wouldn't care. He doesn't care about anything since Theresa passed on. She was all he had. The parents drank, and they fought, and they beat their kids. It was a terrible thing."

In the silence I could hear Taylor's young voice. "Kokom, can I make a dress for my doll out of this silvery cloth or is it too good?"

Kokom said something too soft and low for me to hear, but they both laughed.

I turned back to Beth Mirasty. "Did they live around here? Theresa's family?"

"In town. In a kind of shack on the outskirts. They burned it down one night when they were drinking."

"What did they do?" I said.

She shrugged. "They found another shack."

For a while we were silent again. Then Beth Mirasty said, "When I wrote to you, I said I needed to know if Theresa was happy at the last. Before her accident."

"Her accident." I had used the phrase "tragically and accidentally" to describe Christy's death in her obituary; the newspaper had never reported that Christy committed suicide. Beth Mirasty didn't know the truth. Her brown eyes were intent; I could feel the tension in her body.

I remembered that last day. Christy running across the lawn, hugging me, smelling of soap and sunshine and cotton. "I've missed this family," she had said. And later, she had stood in front of a field white with tundra swans, splitting the air with their plaintive cries as they migrated north. "If they're smart and they're lucky, they'll make it," she had said. It was best to end the movie there.

I took the photo from Beth Mirasty's hands. "Yes," I said, "Theresa was happy at the end."

Somewhere a clock struck. I looked at my watch. "I guess it's time for me to leave. I have to get my boy up to camp."

"I'll walk down to the dock with you," Beth said.

When we came through the clearing in the bush to the lake, I could feel my breath catch in my throat. Havre Lake was one of those northern lakes that is so vast it makes your mind stop. There is something anarchic about such lakes. They make their own weather and have their own intricate geography of islands and points and narrows through which they reach out into other unimaginably vast bodies of water. They exist on maps as huge, whimsically shaped expanses of nothing in the middle of the neat cartography of the places we know.

Angus and Beth's son were fishing off the dock.

When he heard me, Angus turned and held up the fingers of one hand.

"Five minutes, Mum, please, just five. There's a jack in there that's so ready to be caught," he whispered.

"Five, and that's it," I said.

Beth and I walked down to the beach and stood side by side, looking out at the horizon.

"I always feel scared when I look at these lakes," I said.

"Can't you swim?" she asked.

"Yes," I said, "but that's not good enough here, is it?"

"No," she agreed, "it's not." She pointed toward the west. "That's where you're going, Blue Heron Point. When we were growing up, the only store was over there. Then they built the hotel. Now it's a little town. Not a very nice one.

"Anyway, when we were young, that was the treat, getting in the boat once a month before freeze-up and going across the lake to the store. Theresa used to take money out of her father's pocket when he passed out, and she'd take the boat over there herself to get food for her and her brother. Sometimes when it got worse than usual at home, she'd stop on one of the islands and she and Jackie would stay there until the groceries ran out. Just sleeping on the ground. Kokom would make my dad take blankets out for them to lie on, and they'd be safe for a while. But they always had to come to shore.

"I'll never forget watching that little girl start out across the big lake with Jackie sitting beside her. Two little dots in the boat, so small, until the boat was just a dot, and then it disappeared."

I was relieved when I heard Angus shouting that he'd caught a fish. Beth Mirasty's memories of Theresa's childhood were taking me to a place I didn't want to be.

Angus landed his jackfish, and it was a beauty. Beth offered to clean it and freeze it so we could pick it up on the way home. As we walked toward the Northern Lights Motel, Angus was ecstatic. The boys ran on ahead with the fish. I turned to Beth.

"Does Theresa's brother still live around here?"

"He lives in Blue Heron Point."

"Do you have an address?"

"Whatever pub opens first for the day." She shook her head with annoyance. "It's such a waste. He comes over here to eat sometimes if he hasn't hocked his boat to buy a bottle. When he's sober, he's as good a guide as there is. Theresa taught him. But when he's drinking, he's just another drunk. If you want to talk to him, be sure to get there in the first hour after the bar opens. Before that he's too sick with wanting it, and then after that he's just sick."

Beth stopped at the back of the motel with the boys. She sent her son inside for a knife. She said to Angus, "You might as well learn to do this now. Your mother can go and get your sister."

Taylor had a lap full of dolls. With their painted faces, their bright scraps of skirts and their wishbone legs, they were odd and very lovely.

"Dynamite dolls, T.," I said, and meant it.

Kokom said to Taylor, "In my room is a red box that had candy in it. A heart box. You can have it for your dollies."

Taylor ran off. When she was safely out of the room, I heard the old lady's voice.

"That Desjarlais girl. Let her rest in peace now. She's been wandering all her life."

I felt a chill. I turned. The old lady was sewing on her quilt again. I hadn't noticed before how badly her fingers had been gnarled by arthritis, but her needle never stopped. She didn't look up.

"The parents were no good," she said. "When she was young like your little one here, the parents used to leave her with the babies. There were two babies then. The family had a big dog, female. The kids used to play with it. One day in the spring that female dog was in season. There were wild dogs or maybe wolves. They must have smelled the female dog on that little kid. They came and tore that baby to bits. It was a terrible thing. The parents blamed Theresa. They beat her something terrible. She brought her brother and stayed with us for a while. We wanted to keep her, but they said no."

"How did she ever get away?" I said. I was really thinking aloud, but the old lady answered me. Her voice was strong and filled with anger.

"She didn't. The wild dogs got her, too. Let her rest. It doesn't matter any more."

It didn't take long to get Angus settled in at camp. As soon as he jumped out of the car, he saw two boys he had known from the summer before. They came over and grabbed his gear, and the three of them disappeared.

"Goodbye," I shouted after him.

He ran back and gave Taylor a quick hug.

"Please don't kiss me, Mum," he said under his breath.

I gave him a manly pat on the back. "See you in two weeks," I said. I took Taylor's hand. "Looks like it's just you and me against the world, kiddo. What do you want for supper?"

"Cheeseburgers," she said.

"The north is famous for its cheeseburgers," I said.

The drive into Blue Heron Point was not a pretty one. There'd been forest fires in the area the year before, and the charred trunks of trees rose spectral against the summer sky. On the rocky faces of the hills kids had spray-painted messages: "OKA NOW," "CARLA RULES," "CLASS OF 91 NO FUTUR." Blue Heron Point was the kind of northern town that exists for the people who come to fish. All the buildings faced out on the dirt road that followed the shoreline. There were two inns, a couple of motels, and, set back from the road, the Kingfisher Hotel. They all had bars, and they all had no-vacancy signs. There were two general stores with restaurants, and a liquor store.

"Which place looks best to eat, T.?" I said.

"The one with the dogs fighting outside," she said.

In fact, the food was good and plentiful: a homemade cheeseburger and a dinner plate filled with greasy, salty French fries.

After we finished, I said, "Now for the hard part, finding a place to stay. I wish I'd asked Greg's uncle if we could use his cottage."

"But you didn't," Taylor said, twirling a fry in her ketchup.

"Nope, it didn't work out," I said. "Let me go and ask at the counter what they suggest. I'm too tired to drive any more today. Besides, there's someone I want to try to find here."

I looked at my watch. Six o'clock. According to Beth's calculations, Jackie Desjarlais would have been drinking for six hours. Tomorrow would be better.

The woman at the cash register was not encouraging. It was the Tuesday after the long weekend, and a lot of people take their holidays the first two weeks in July. I paid for our lunch, thanked her and started to leave. She called me back.

"You could ask at the hotel about the fishing shacks," she said. "They're awfully small, but they're clean and they're right on the lake. Pretty views."

The man behind the desk at the hotel was huge. He was wearing a T-shirt that said, "Jackfish in Lard Makes a Fisherman Hard." When I asked about a room, he opened the registration book, ran a thick finger down the page and then grinned at me.

"You're damn lucky, lady. There's one unit left. Last empty bed in town. Twenty bucks. Pay now. The money's up front for the shacks. I've put you in number three."

The shacks were, in fact, one building, which must have been built before the province had passed its law about not building directly on lakefront property. The place was right down by the docks. It was old and had the frail, stripped-down look of wartime housing. The individual units were tiny, just one small room and a bathroom, but each unit had a small kitchen and a large window that opened onto a screened-in porch. It was obvious that they were a place to sleep for people who wanted to fish.

Taylor was enchanted. "It's like a doll's house," she said, opening the little refrigerator and pulling out an ice tray that made six cubes.

We unpacked and then we went for a swim. When we'd changed out of our swimsuits, we sat on the dock and watched the boats come in. A sunburned man with a tub full of fish asked Taylor if she'd had any luck.

"Yes," she said, "I got to stay in the little house up there." She pointed toward the shacks.

He laughed. "That makes us neighbours. I'm staying there, too."

Nice. We had supper at the hotel, and after we ate, I decided to call Jill Osiowy to give her the hotel's number in case there were any changes about our July eighth show. It was almost seven, but she was still at her office. She answered on the first ring, and she sounded tense and distracted.

"You sound as if you could use a little down time in the north yourself," I said.

"Sorry," she said, "but I have company. Con O'Malley and his Corporate Choir Boys. It's been years since I've seen that many pinstriped suits."

"You didn't mention you were having a royal visit," I said.

"I didn't know," she said. "They just arrived two hours ago. I was editing some of the Little Flower tapes – on my own time, of course – and my secretary called and said we'd been invaded. I haven't the slightest idea what they're doing here."

"Spooking you," I said.

"You've got that right," she said. "I'm spooked. CEOs are like cops. Even when you know you haven't done anything wrong, you'd rather they weren't around. Listen, Jo, I'd better go. I'll call you tomorrow night."

I gave her the hotel number and hung up. Taylor and I walked down the hill to the shacks. It was such a beautiful night that we stayed on the dock until sunset. I looked out at the lake and watched Taylor's small silhouette black against the red sky and the dropping sun. How many nights had

Theresa Desjarlais stood on the shore of Havre Lake and watched as the sun dropped in the sky and the water turned to fire? Finally, when the darkness closed in on us, Taylor and I walked to our cabin.

There was just one double bed. It felt good to lie there on the cool smooth sheets with Taylor's body curled against me. Her hair smelled of heat and lake water, and I closed my eyes and remembered holding Mieka in just this way when she was small, and the boys, too, when they were little. I touched the silver circle of my bracelet and remembered Christy. "Did anyone ever hold you like this when you were little, Christy-Theresa?" I said. "Did anyone ever encircle you in close and protective arms?" And because I knew the answer, I wept.

CHAPTER

11

When the boy appeared outside the shack's screen door saying there was a phone call for me up at the Kingfisher, Taylor and I were just finishing dinner. On the table between us was a map of Havre Lake; we were planning the boat trip we were taking the next morning. It had been a good day. We'd walked the shoreline from Blue Heron Point to Hampton Narrows, an hour and a half away, and Taylor had found a piece of driftwood shaped like a bird, some fool's gold, and the torso of a Barbie doll. Serendipity.

She'd had more luck than I'd had. As soon as I knew the bars were open, I'd started checking around for Jackie Desjarlais. No one had seen him. In the last place we tried, the bartender told me Jackie had been blind drunk the night before, and if I had anything serious to say to him I'd be smart to wait until the next day.

At some level, I had been relieved. The prospect of a day without sadness or ugliness was appealing. Cut loose from responsibilities, Taylor and I had given ourselves up to the pleasures of cottage life. We went down to the beach for a swim, then we sat on blankets on the sand and let the breeze dry us off. At midafternoon, we walked to the store in Blue Heron Point and bought supplies: groceries, matches for fire starting, a bottle of sun block and a jar of blackfly repellent guaranteed to be environmentally friendly. On the way out of the store, Taylor picked up a baseball cap with the words "I'd Rather Be Fishing" written in fish across the front.

"It's to keep the sun off my head," she said. "Angus says too much sun can boil your brains."

She'd put the hat on the coat hook by the door the way Angus always did at home, and that night as we followed the boy out of the cabin, she reached up, grabbed her cap and jammed it over her hair.

"Nice hat," the boy said, and Taylor beamed. They talked about fishing all the way up to the hotel.

I went inside. The man who had checked us in was sitting on a stool behind the front desk. He handed me a message slip with a number I recognized as Jill Oziowy's.

"The lady said to call her back reverse the charges." He slid the phone across the desk to me. "I'm here to make sure those charges get reversed."

Jill sounded edgy and excited. "Things are happening, Jo," she said. "Last night when I finally got home, there was a message on my answering service. A man's voice, muffled. 'Check out the Lily Pad,' he said, and hung up. Just like in the movies. It was after midnight, and I was dead tired. Those little trolls from head office had been nipping at my heels all night, so I didn't go over to the Lily Pad till about seven this morning. Guess what? The place was closed up tighter than a drum, padlock on the front door, blinds drawn. There were two kids on the lawn by that wooden frog, but they were so pilled up I don't think they knew where they were.

"I went around and checked out the back. Same thing. Incidentally, you were right about that door, Jo, that's a serious security system. I just don't understand what it's doing there. Why would the Lily Pad people tie up that kind of money in the back door of a drop-in centre for street kids?"

"Because it's something more than a drop-in centre," I said. The manager hadn't moved from his stool. He was less than two feet away from me. As soon as my call to Jill had gone through, he'd pulled out a pair of scissors and started cleaning his nails. When I mentioned the drop-in centre, he stopped digging and looked up at me with quick and interested eyes.

I lowered my voice. "I can't talk here," I said.

"I'll talk," Jill said. "I remembered what you said about Helmut Keating taking all that liquor in on Saturday. I thought the kids on the lawn might have heard something. At first, I thought I was out of luck. Whatever drug those kids had been doing had propelled them to another dimension, but I just kept talking, and when I mentioned Helmut Keating's name, I got a reaction. One of the boys pulled himself together enough to get out a full sentence: 'They say Helmie blew town,' he said. What do you make of that, Jo?"

"Interesting," I said, and I smiled at the hotel manager. He didn't smile back.

"Keating's not in the book, but I called a friend of mine who's also into good works and she had an address for him. Jo, you wouldn't have believed his house. A big split level out on Academy Park Road."

"The dysfunctional population business must be pretty lucrative," I said.

"Right," said Jill. "But listen, Helmie's place was shut tight, blinds pulled. The neighbour was out watering her lawn and she said Helmut took off this morning, very early, in a cab. He had suitcases. That's all she knew. Jo, it's just a hunch, but I think Helmut Keating was my mystery caller. I think he's decided to blow the whistle on the Lily Pad. I'm going to make some calls to people I know at the airport and the bus station. See if I can track down our travelling man. Then I'm going back to the Lily Pad. There may be a kid there who's kept her eyes open and her brain unfried."

She swore softly. "I've lost a whole day, but there was no way around it. My new best friends from head office insisted on getting an early start. On what, I still haven't figured out. Jo, I was tracking down stuff for them all day, figures, employment records, old interviews. And whatever I got wasn't enough, they'd just send me off again. I felt like that girl in the fairy tale who had to keep spinning straw into gold, and no matter how much she spun it was never enough. What was the name of that story anyway?"

"Rumpelstiltskin," I said.

Jill laughed. "Jo, you're so well read. Anyway, after I spent the day spinning my straw, I came home and there was a threat on my machine."

The hotel manager leaned forward; he was so close I could smell his aftershave. It was artificially piny, like the little deodorant trees people hang from the rear-view mirror of cars.

"What kind of threat?" I asked.

"Just a garden-variety death threat," Jill said quietly. "I've heard worse. Anyway, that's where we are now."

"I think you should call the police," I said.

"Not yet," she said. "This one's still mine. Jo, I can feel the adrenaline. Something's coming."

"Be careful," I said. "Please, please, be careful."

I had a troubled sleep that night. I dreamed I was at the back door of the Lily Pad. I could hear a child crying inside, and I was frantic to get in. I had a card for the security system, but every time I tried to use it to open the door, the system spit the card back out at me. No matter how many ways I tried, I couldn't get the card to fit. Then Blaine Harris was there in his ponytail and his beaded moccasins. "The rain," he said urgently. "The rain," I said, and it seemed to be the right thing to say because he smiled at me and gave me an old paper dollar. I put the dollar into the card slot, and the door opened. Then I woke up.

The next morning I was up with the sun; after the puzzling dream of the night before, I was glad to see it. A car pulled into the parking lot in front of the unit next door, and that was reassuring, too. It felt good to be part of the solid world where the sun shines and people come and go. I could hear the voice of our neighbour, the sunburned man who had talked to Taylor when he came in from fishing the night we came. It was obvious that he and the man who had just arrived were old friends who met somewhere every year to fish. As I heard my neighbour and his friend exchange their bluff hearty greetings and run through the familiar litany about the condition of the roads they'd driven and how much booze they'd brought and where the fish were biting, I was smiling. Unreconstructed, unrepentant Real Men. No one needed to give these guys drums to get in touch with their inner selves.

Then the man who had just arrived lowered his voice. "So where's the hairless pussy around here?" he asked.

The sunburned man laughed. "On an island, if you can believe it. You need a fucking guide to take you there, but, sweet Jesus, it's worth it."

Beside me, Taylor, still asleep, rolled over onto her back. She muttered something, then she smiled and stretched out her arms in a gesture of animal trust.

I felt my stomach lurch, and I sat up, tense, alert to danger.

Next door, the sunburned man said, "First things first. Come on in and we'll have an eye-opener."

The screen door slammed. For the next fifteen minutes, as I sat, still and silent, I could hear the low murmur of the voices on the other side of the wall. Finally, the screen door slammed again, and I could hear the men's voices fade as they moved toward the dock. I walked onto our porch and watched until they got into the boat and started the motor. I didn't stop watching until their boat disappeared into the line that separated the blue of the sky from the blue of the lake. I hoped they would drown.

When I went in, Taylor was sitting up with the candy box full of dolls on her knees.

"We're going to the island to make breakfast," she said. "Remember, Jo? You're going to make a fire and we're going to cook bacon. I dreamed about it even."

My heart was pounding so hard I thought it would beat out of my chest. I wanted to take Taylor's hand and run.

Oblivious, Taylor arranged her dolls on the bedspread. "Kokom says on the islands you can find moss that will keep my dolls from breaking when I carry them. She says when she was a girl people used to put that moss around real babies." She looked up at me hopefully. "Jo?"

"Just trying to remember how to make a campfire, T.," I said. "Come on, let's get rolling. Get dressed and we'll pack up our food. I've already looked at the lake this morning. It's like glass. Perfect weather for a shore breakfast."

Three-quarters of an hour later, picnic cooler loaded, Thermos filled, we were fastening our life jackets. It was going to be a great day, hot and still and sun-filled, but the man at the boat rental had been cautious.

"Where you want to go is South Bay," he said. "You'll be okay there. It's close, and on that map of yours, the Xs show where the rocks are. Don't go through the narrows into the lake proper. Too much can go wrong. Hit a rock, get stuck out in the middle when a storm hits, and you and the little girl here will buy it."

I looked at my map; there were a lot of Xs, but it was reassuring, for once, to know where the dangers were.

It had been years since I'd driven a motorboat, but it wasn't a complex skill, and it felt good to put some distance between me and Blue Heron Point. As our boat cut through the shining water, Taylor's eyes were wide, taking in all the sights. When we came to the bay, I cut back the motor. There were perhaps twenty islands to choose from. They weren't the gentle islands of children's books; they were steep, with shirred rock faces that rose sharp and hostile from the water. The treeline was high on these islands, and it wasn't until you climbed to the top that you were protected by bushes and evergreens.

"You pick," I shouted to Taylor over the low hum of the motor. "Which one looks good to you?"

"Can we move closer?" she said.

"Sure," I said, and we moved slowly through the bay, checking them out.

Finally Taylor pointed to one that seemed tucked away behind the others. "That one," she said. "No one will ever find us there."

It was as if she had read my mind.

We pulled the boat up on shore and tied it to a rock. When we were sure it was secure, we climbed up the rock face in search of wood. At the top of the hill the terrain was hospitable, flat and tree-covered. The sun came through the evergreens and made shifting patterns on the moss. I was standing there admiring the view when Taylor called me.

"Look," she said. "People were here before." On a stump between two trees, someone had piled stones and made a little altar. A plastic figure of the virgin was wedged into the stones at the top. On the ground in front of the altar was a ring of stones enclosing the charred remains of a fire.

As I looked at the garish little figurine I thought of Theresa and her brother. Two children on an island. At night it must have been terrifying: the unbroken darkness of the northern sky, the birds swooping to shore, the lake black with secrets. Had Theresa built a fire? Had she found a plastic Mary like this one to mother Jackie and her through the night? So many terrors. But she was a child who was used to terrors.

"Jo? Jo, what're you thinking about?" Taylor was tugging at my hand. "Are you thinking about eating? Because I am."

"Time to make a campfire then," I said.

We built a fire on the rock, and we cooked bacon and made toast and boiled the lake water for tea. The tea tasted of twigs and smoke. After we cleaned our dishes and put out our fire, we explored the island, then we swam in the icy water. Taylor dog-paddled for a while, then she floated on her back and looked at the birds circling in the blue sky. When we got tired, we came ashore and lay in the sun on towels stretched over the rocks.

With the sun hot on my back, the warm rock under me and the sound of birdsong in the air, the tension seeped out of my body, and I drifted off to sleep. I awoke to feel my bracelet burning from the sun. Taylor was sitting on her towel, carefully arranging the moss she'd collected around her wishbone dolls.

"You were sleeping," she said with a smile.

I looked at my watch. It was twenty to twelve. By the time I got back to shore and changed, the pubs would have been open half an hour. With luck, Jackie Desjarlais would be ready to talk.

As we tied the boat to the dock in front of the shacks, I decided I'd try the Kingfisher first. That way I could check for phone messages, too. Taylor and I dropped our picnic gear at our cabin and walked up the hill to the hotel. The steps were filled with blank-faced kids smoking – Lily Pad north. When I asked if anyone had seen Jackie Desjarlais that day, they didn't even bother looking up, and as we went up the steps, Taylor and I had to walk carefully to keep from stepping on them.

It wasn't hard to find the bar. A plastic muskellunge arced over the doorway to a dark and cavernous room. Burned into a block of cedar under the fish were the words "Angler's Corner." It was only half an hour after opening, but already the pine room deodorizer was losing out to the smells of stale beer and cigarettes and urine. I waited for my eyes to adjust to the darkness, then Taylor and I started across the room. We didn't get far. I hadn't taken three steps when a hand reached out from behind me and closed around my upper arm.

"You can't be in here with a kid." The man behind me was huge and menacing; they grow their bouncers big in the north.

"I'm not staying," I said. "I'm just looking for someone."

His hand didn't relax its grip.

"I'm looking for Jackie Desjarlais," I said.

He looked at me stonily.

"Can you help me?" I said.

"If I see him, I'll tell him you're lookin'," he said, and he started pushing me toward the door.

"Tell him I'm a friend of Theresa's," I said. "My name is Joanne and I'm staying at the shacks down by the lake."

By the time I finished the sentence, I was out the front door, blinking in the sunlight.

I had just started down the steps when I heard someone call my name. I turned and I was face to face with Jackie Desjarlais. I would have known him anywhere. He was, as my grandmother would have said, the dead spit of his sister: the same slight body, the same dark eyes, the same wide, generous mouth. Except that everything that was fluid and graceful in her had gone slack in him.

I smiled at him. "Hello, Jackie," I said.

"You know me?" he asked, surprised.

"You look so much like her," I said.

"No," he said, "she was beautiful."

Unexpectedly, his eyes filled with tears. He lit a cigarette and began to cough. He coughed so hard that he bent over double; finally, he straightened and wiped his lips and eyes.

"Fuck," he said. "These things are goin' to fuckin' kill me." For the first time he noticed Taylor. "I'm sorry," he said to her.

She moved toward him. "It's okay. My brother Angus says that, too."

Despite everything, I felt a warmth. "My brother Angus." The words sounded good.

Jackie's face seemed to open a little.

I touched his arm. "Talk to me," I said. "Tell me about Theresa. She was my son's girlfriend, but I never really got to know her."

"I know who you are," he said. "Terry showed me the Christmas pictures."

"You must have been so proud of her," I said.

He looked at me as if I was insane. "Proud?" He repeated the word uncomprehendingly.

"Proud of all she accomplished. Going to university. Putting the sadness she knew here behind her. How did she get out of here, Jackie? Tell me."

He drew deeply on his cigarette and blew a careful smoke ring. "There's only one way for girls to get out of here," he said. "I got nothin' more to say."

He opened the door to the hotel. Somewhere in that stale-aired darkness Dan Seals was singing "All That Glitters Is Not Gold." Jackie looked at Taylor. For the first time, he smiled. His smile was Theresa's smile. As his mouth curved into that familiar mocking line, my heart lurched. He reached into his pocket, pulled out a loonie and handed the coin to Taylor.

"Little Sister," he said, and he turned and walked through the door.

I guess I had known how Theresa Desjarlais became Christy Sinclair from the moment I saw the bleak sandy streets of Blue Heron Point: no businesses or offices where a young girl could work to earn enough money to get away, just hotels and bars where women's work was menial and permanent.

As Taylor and I walked down the incline from the hotel, I felt leaden. Taylor's hand was small in mine, something to hold on to. The rain started when we were halfway down the hill. Just a few drops at first, then more, closer together. By the time we reached the fishing shacks the heavens had opened, the wind had picked up, and there were whitecaps on the lake.

Taylor and I were soaked to the skin. We got inside, towelled off and changed into dry clothes. Taylor pulled down the bedspread and crawled into bed.

"I didn't sleep on the island, Jo," she said. "I had to watch."

I sat at the table by the window, listened to the rain pounding into the turbulent lake and thought about the lonely life of Christy Sinclair.

She had been a prostitute. The little girl who had been beaten by her drunken parents had used her only asset to get out. Somewhere between Blue Heron Point and the University of Saskatchewan, where Peter met her, Theresa Desjarlais had transformed herself. She'd become educated, learned how to dress, changed her name. She'd walked away from everything that made her a victim, started a new life. She'd escaped.

At least for a while. But the past was there, as permanent as the teddy bear tattoo on her left buttock, the teddy bear tattoo that was the same as Bernice Morin's. And then . . . And then what? Christy had walked into Mieka's store one afternoon, and Bernice Morin had been there. What had happened after that?

I was so deep in thought that I guess I didn't hear him knocking. Finally, frustrated and soaked to the skin, he opened the door. It was the boy who had delivered the message the night before. He was wearing a bright neon shirt and a cap like the one of Taylor's he'd admired so much.

I smiled and told him I liked his hat, but he didn't smile back. He was solemn with the importance of his message. "There's a phone call at the hotel for you. An emergency, they said, for Joanne. They sent me to get you. Quick."

I looked at Taylor sleeping, warm in her bed, and I looked at the rain outside.

I decided in a second.

I grabbed my bag, took out a five-dollar bill and handed it to the boy. "You remember Taylor. Stay with her for a while, will you? I don't want to take her out in this, and she'll be scared if she wakes up and I'm gone."

His hand shot out and grabbed the five dollars.

"I'll give you five more if you're here when I get back," I said.

"I'll be here," he said, sitting down at the kitchen table.

I grabbed my jacket. It wasn't much use against a rain that seemed torrential, but it was something. As I climbed the hill, the gravel gave way beneath my feet. It seemed I took one step forward and slid back two. The whole summer had been like that – filled with frustration, filled with rain, filled with death. I was glad to see the soft fuzz of light from the hotel through the grey. I ran across the parking lot. Incredibly, the kids were still sitting on the steps. A couple of the more sober ones were holding green plastic garbage bags over their heads as protection, but the rest were so drunk they didn't seem to realize it was raining. A girl was standing at the side of the steps vomiting. I could hear her retching as I ran past her into the hotel.

The hotel manager was wearing the shirt he'd been wearing the night Taylor and I arrived, the one that said, "Jackfish in Lard Makes a Fisherman Hard."

"There's a message for me," I said. "An emergency phone call."

"Says who?" He was smiling, enjoying his role as rustic funny man. This was going to be rich.

"The boy who brought the message last night came by the fishing shacks a few minutes ago. A little guy about ten, wearing a neon T-shirt and a new cap."

"He must've been playing a joke," the proprietor said.

"A joke?" I said.

"Yeah, a joke." His face rearranged itself into a mask of concern. "Of course, he could be a thief. These kids around here learn fast. If you've got valuables in that shack, you might be smart to hightail it back there. This hotel is not liable for anything that gets taken from a guest's room. You're warned. There's a sign on your door."

"There aren't any valuables there," I said. And then I thought of Taylor. Taylor was there.

For a split second I considered asking him to help me. Then I looked into his eyes. He wouldn't have crossed the room to save his own mother. I was on my own. I ran down the hill, slipping in the loose wet gravel, catching myself on bush branches to keep from falling. I ran and fell and picked myself up and ran again. I went as fast as I could, but it wasn't fast enough. The front door to the shack was open. There was no one at the table. There was no one in the bed.

I called her name. I called and called, but as I sank down in the chair at the kitchen table, I knew she couldn't hear me.

I ran outside and looked along the shoreline. It was deserted. I thought I saw a boat heading through the north channel, but it was raining so hard I wasn't sure. I tried to listen for the sound of a motor, but it was no use.

As I walked to the shack, I could feel the panic rising. I opened the screen door and went in. "This is how it starts," I said, and my voice echoed in the empty room. "This is how it starts."

In the mirror above the dresser, I could see myself. My hair was dark with rain, and my face was wet, but I looked like my ordinary self. I thought of the dozens of times I had seen the parents of abducted children on television. For all of them, the nightmare must have started just like this, on an ordinary day when, just for a moment, they had dropped their guard, and everything had changed forever. They had been ordinary people living anonymous lives, and then, in the blink of an eye, they were famous, their tense faces flickering across our television sets, their voices breaking as they justified themselves to the audience. "I only turned my back for a second; she was right there." "We never left him alone." "I always told him not to talk to strangers."

After the media wearied of their stories, the lost children's pictures cropped up on bus shelters and milk cartons. And I would look at the pictures of these children, faces shining, hair freshly cut for the school photographer, and tell myself this wouldn't have happened if the parents had been careful. This wouldn't have happened if the parents had been conscientious; if they had really loved their kids; if they hadn't taken chances. It was a mantra to distance myself, protect myself, and it had worked for twenty-one years.

Now, without warning, I had crossed the line that separates the lucky ones from the losers. Now I would be the one on TV, and it would be Taylor's picture that would be . . . A thought struck me, terrible, annihilating. I didn't have a picture of Taylor. She had only been with us since February. I hadn't taken her picture. I wasn't a good parent. I was negligent.

Without a picture, I could lose her forever. I could forget her face, and it would be as if she had never existed. Suddenly, finding a picture was the most important thing. There had to be one somewhere. My mind spun crazily through the possibilities. And then, I remembered.

The new bike. The morning we bought her new bike, I had taken pictures of Taylor wobbling down the driveway. I remembered looking through the view finder and noticing that the pink stripe on her safety helmet was exactly the shade of pink on her two-wheeler.

I hadn't failed her, after all. Suddenly, as if it had appeared as a reward for my diligence, I saw the postcard. It was on top of the dresser. The printing looked hurried. "Don't call the police for 24 hours and she'll be back safe." I turned it over; on the other side there was a picture of the Kingfisher Hotel, seductive under picture-book turquoise skies.

Twenty-four hours . . . I began to shake at the thought of what they could do to her in twenty-four hours. I thought about the men next door. "So where's the hairless pussy around here?" My stomach heaved, but I pushed myself up from the table and walked next door. Their car was still out back, but they could have taken her in a boat. A boat would have been the thing. They could have taken her out in the channel to the big lake, to the islands where you couldn't hear a child screaming. Their screen door was unlatched. I went onto the porch and pounded on their front door. There was no answer, but I had to be sure. I tried to smash down the door, but it was surprisingly solid. They had left the front window open an inch. Only the screen protected it, but when I tried to loosen the screen by hand, it wouldn't budge. Years of paint had stuck it firm. I went back to our place and picked up a butcher knife. I used the knife to cut through the screen and I reached in and raised the window. I crawled through onto the kitchen table. There was no one there.

Their suitcases were open on the floor. I started rummaging in them, looking for something that might help me know what had happened. The cases were filled with clothes for the fishermen. Someone had bought these things for a man who was a husband and father. ("This will be a good shirt for Dad when he goes up north.") At the bottom of the suitcases were the magazines. They were unspeakable. Think of the worst thing you know, and this was worse. The children looked as if they had been drugged. I hoped to God they had been drugged, anything so they wouldn't feel the things that were being done to their bodies, those fragile, perfect bodies.

When I looked at the magazines, I knew there was a connection between this perversion and Taylor's disappearance. And I knew something else. Everything was connected somehow to the Lily Pad. But how? As I climbed the hill to the hotel, I repeated the word, pounding it into the ground with every leaden footstep.

This time I didn't use the phone in the hotel. There was a pay phone outside the restaurant where Taylor and I had eaten that first night. I went into the restaurant and got change, then I came back out and called Jill Osiowy.

She answered on the first ring. "They've taken Taylor," I said. "They left a postcard with instructions. They say if I don't call the police, they'll bring her back safe in twenty-four hours."

"Do what they say," Jill said. Her voice was dead. "Jo, Helmut Keating called. The people who own the Lily Pad are after him. He found out something about Kim Barilko's murder, and he got greedy. He says they're going to kill him. Jo, I believe him. He wants me to get into their computer. He says if I key in the word 'teddy,' I'll get everything I need. I can stop them, Jo. I can stop those bastards."

Suddenly, Jill's voice broke. "Do you know what they did? They killed Murray and Lou. They slit their throats and dropped them in my garbage can."

There were black spots in front of my eyes, and my knees went weak. I thought I was going to pass out. I opened the door to the telephone booth and took deep breaths till the faintness passed.

All the time, Jill was talking to me. "Jo, do what they say about Taylor. Don't call the police. Don't take a chance with her."

The line went dead. For a moment my options flashed wildly through my mind. There weren't many. I thought of Jill's old tortoiseshell-cats, killed as a warning, and I knew I wasn't going to leave Taylor with those monsters for twenty-four hours.

When I walked through the door to the Angler's Corner, I was cold with anger. No one was going to hurt Taylor. Jackie Desjarlais was in the corner playing pool. I grabbed his arm and started dragging him toward the door.

"You're coming with me," I said.

"Are you crazy?" he said.

I jerked him toward me till our faces were almost touching. "Do I look crazy?" I said.

"Yeah," he said, "you do." He tried to wrench away from me.

"Someone's taken Taylor," I said, "and I think they're going to hurt her."

"Little Sister," he said.

He had been drinking, but he wasn't drunk.

"I think they've taken her somewhere in the lake. To an island. I need you to –"

"The Lily Pad," he said.

I felt as if I'd stepped through the looking glass.

His voice was dead. "The Lily Pad. That's where Theresa

was. It's a place where men can do things to kids. Theresa said it was just a business. That's how much they fucked her over. That she would think it was just a business."

"Please," I said.

"Let's go," he said. "My boat's down at the dock. You got money for gas? I drank my last five bucks."

"I've got money," I said.

When he came back, he had a gas can and a bottle of rye. His boat was a new one, fibreglass with a fifty-horsepower outboard motor. It looked sturdy. Then I looked out at the lake, and suddenly Jackie's boat seemed very small. He reached under the front and pulled out a khaki slicker.

"Put this on," he said. He opened the rye. "Take a slug."

I did. The whisky burned my throat, but it warmed and calmed me.

It took us forty-five minutes to get to the island, forty-five minutes of being pounded by the storm and my own fear. We were heading into the wind and the rain was blinding. Every time Jackie's boat slapped against the whitecaps, it shuddered as if it was about to split in two. My panic about Taylor hit in waves, overwhelming me. At one point, I looked out and I couldn't see anything: no islands, no shoreline, no line dividing earth from heaven. In that moment I felt a stab of existential terror. I was alone in the universe in a frail boat with a stranger. It was a metaphor the psalmist would have understood.

And then Jackie Desjarlais looked up and smiled at me.

"Some fun," he said.

"Yeah," I said, "some fun."

Those were the only words we spoke until the island came into view. The rain had stopped, and as we came closer to shore, I turned to Jackie.

"Shouldn't we try to keep out of sight?" I asked.

"They know the boat," he said flatly.

For a moment, I thought I'd fallen into a trap. I remembered Jill Osiowy's warning: "Don't take things at face value. For once in your life, Jo, don't assume the best."

"Everybody here works for them one way or another," Jackie was saying. "I'm one of the ones that brings the clients over." He shuddered. "And I feel like shit. Theresa always said it was a business, a service. You asked me back there how she got out of Blue Heron Point. She worked for them. She started when she was a kid. Maybe eleven. She didn't have no choice then. Our old man was a drunken son of a bitch and our mother . . ." He spat into the water. He looked at me and his eyes were dark with fury. "Our mother was no mother. A woman from town told Theresa that Social Services was going to take me and her, too, unless Theresa did something. So she did something . . ."

"She must have loved you very much," I said.

"She woulda done anything for me," he said flatly. "When she was older, they brought her into the business. They sent her down south to go to high school and look for more kids. For a couple of years she was a kind of manager at their place in Regina. She made a lotta money, bought me this boat, bought me everything. She always took care of me." His voice broke. "Fuck," he said.

We were almost ashore. He wiped his eyes with the sleeve of his jacket. I looked into my bag for a Kleenex, and there, folded neatly, forgotten, was the picture Taylor had drawn the morning after Theresa died.

I closed my eyes and remembered how Taylor had looked, running down the hill, hair tangled from sleep, laughing, eager to get the day started. And she had drawn this. I unfolded it and felt the tears come.

Frogs. Dozens of frogs, big and little, smiling and sad, dozens of frogs for Angus because I wouldn't let him take any home to the city with us.

We were almost ashore. Through the trees I could see the outline of a low building that looked like a motel. I started to fold up Taylor's frog picture. There was writing on the back of the page. The writing was familiar. I had seen it on the front of a hundred shell-pink envelopes the night Lorraine Harris and I addressed the wedding invitations. Here, in her familiar looping backhand, were the names of the players on the croquet teams the night of the engagement party.

The Jacks: Joanne, Keith, Angus, Taylor.

The Aces: Peter Kilbourn, Theresa, Mieka, Greg.

I read the names again. She had written "Theresa," not "Christy." It was impossible. That night none of us knew who Christy Sinclair really was. Except Lorraine Harris had known.

With a jolt, the boat hit the dock and Jackie jumped ashore.

For a moment, I didn't move.

Jackie Desjarlais must have seen the bewilderment in my face. He reached his hand out and pulled me ashore.

"Come on," he said gently. "It's time to go get Little Sister."

CHAPTER

12

As we moved from the dock to the shelter of the trees, I felt as if I was in a dream. As suddenly as it had begun, the wind had stopped, and there was a preternatural calm on the island. The air was dense with moisture, and as we moved toward the building, the ground was spongy beneath our feet. In the motionless air, every leaf and stone was thrown into sharp relief. It was a hushed and menacing world.

I leaned close to Jackie Desjarlais. "Where would they have her in there?" I asked. "Is there some sort of security?"

Jackie shrugged. "A guy I know says they don't need much because of being on an island. He works there nights sometimes, in case things get out of hand. But from what I've seen, during the day it's pretty much just the girls."

"Then we could go in and take Taylor," I said.

"I don't think that'd be a smart move," he said. "Let me check things out in there first." He took the flask of whisky out of his jacket pocket and held it to his lips. Then he offered it to me.

"Later," I said. "After we get her back."

He started to put the cap on the bottle, then he changed his mind. He poured some rye into his hand and patted it on his cheeks as if it was aftershave. Then he wiped his hand on the front of his shirt.

"My disguise," he said. "Nobody worries about a drunk. I oughta know." He slid the bottle carefully into the inside pocket of his jacket. "I'm gonna go in there and make a stink. It won't be the first time. Anyway, if there's security, that'll flush 'em out. At least we'll know what we're dealing with. Unless you got a different idea."

I shook my head.

"Okay," he said. "Stay outta sight till I get back. Then, if it looks good, we'll both go in."

I watched him lope across the clearing between the trees and the building; his legs were as long and as graceful as Theresa's. The sun came out, pale through the clouds. It seemed like a good omen. I walked among the trees until the Lily Pad was in my line of vision. Taylor was in there. I was sure of it.

The building looked reassuringly ordinary, like a motel or a private club. It was made of cedar, low-slung, sprawling, ranch style. There were a few windows; all were placed high, but there were skylights set into the roof, so there would have been light inside. I seemed to be standing at the side of the building. I moved around so I could see the back. There was a tennis court there, and playground equipment: a jungle gym, a swing set, a teeter-totter. I thought of someone ordering that gym set. ("No, it's not for my own children, it's for company.") The banality of evil. That's what Hannah Arendt had called her book about the men at the top of the Third Reich. The men who came here would be like those men, good to their dogs, fond of gardening, devoted fathers, even, and yet . . . I remembered the magazine photographs I had seen a little more than an hour ago, and my stomach clenched. What dark fantasies had been acted out on those swings? On that jungle gym?

A woman came from the front of the house and began walking toward the tennis court. She was pushing an industrial broom, the kind people use to sweep the water off a court after a rainstorm. Everything about the woman was shapeless: her body in its flowered cotton dress was a mass of shifting contours; her bare legs were pale and lumpy; her ankles were thick and swollen; even the way she walked, with the shambling gait of the lifelong alcoholic, lacked definition. Give this sad woman a bottle a day, and she wouldn't question anything.

Things were starting to come into focus. The elaborate security system on the back door of the Lily Pad in Regina. The locked doors to the upstairs. (Not safe, Kim had told me, the kids might smoke up there. It was a fire hazard.) But it wasn't fire the people who ran the Lily Pad were afraid of. They recruited from the street kids, lured them with the promise of a good life. ("Theresa was going to teach me about clothes and hair," Kim said, her face transformed, "and we were going to talk about going back to school. She had this business, and she was going to train me . . .")

A business. It sounded so innocent, like a bed and breakfast. I remembered the shining kitchen in the Lily Pad on Albert Street, so out of sync with the rest of that mismatched furniture scrounged from the Sally Ann. Then I remembered Helmut Keating trying to keep me from seeing a twenty-pound roast thawing in a pan on the counter. Prime rib. Nothing but the best for the Lily Pad's customers.

How many Lily Pads were there? I thought of the water lilies in the pond by our cottage when I was young. The flowers were beautiful, white and luminous, but when I looked underneath I could see they grew from thick, creeping stems that were buried in the mud at the bottom of the stagnant water. They slimed my hands when I touched them.

I heard a door slam, and Jackie came stumbling around the corner, a parody of a drunk. He picked up speed as he came toward me.

"There's nothing but the girls there. We're okay. I've been trying to come up with something. How does this sound? I go back up there and get everybody crazy and you try the doors at the back of the house. Start with the one closest to us. It's a kind of storeroom. I've delivered booze there sometimes. No one ever seems to worry much about locking it. The locks are on the side where they keep the kids."

I felt a rush of adrenaline. I wanted to find the people who had put the locks on those doors.

Jackie reached into the inside pocket of his jacket. When he pulled his hand out, he was holding a gun. "I sort of borrowed this from the guy who sold me the gas for the boat. He keeps it around in case of trouble. I figured we were more likely to have trouble today than him." He held the gun out to me. "You take it," he said. "If things get hot, just wave it around. Guns scare the shit out of people."

As I took the gun, my hand was trembling. "They scare the shit out of me," I said.

Jackie looked at me levelly. "You'll be all right," he said. He pointed to the woman sweeping the tennis courts. "As soon as she leaves, we'll go in."

It seemed like forever, and as we stood in the breathless mugginess of a July afternoon, I was half crazy with the thought of Taylor alone – or worse, not alone – in that malignant place. Jackie's gun, a dead weight in the pocket of my slicker, seemed to grow heavier as the minutes ticked by.

Finally, the woman picked up her broom and went toward the front of the house. As soon as she was out of sight, I curled my fingers around the handle of the gun and ran across the clearing. The first door at the back was metal, but it had been propped open with a wedge of wood. I opened it and found myself in a storage room. It was all very domestic and disarming. Facing me were two restaurant-size upright freezers. Next to them, in a kind of bin, were sacks of vegetables. Cartons of liquor were neatly stacked against the wall farthest from the door. There was a whole wall of canned goods. When I saw a low shelf near the front filled with tins of Spaghettios, I could feel the anger rising in my throat. I moved cautiously through the storeroom until I came to the kitchen. It was sleek and deserted.

The door was open and I could hear raised voices. One of the voices was male, demanding money, hollering obscenities. Jackie Desjarlais was putting on quite a performance.

I stood, tense, alert, trying to get a sense of the layout of the building. I moved quietly toward the voices and then at the first corridor I turned. Terrified I would make a mistake, I almost did.

She seemed to fly out of the door across from me. If she hadn't been looking toward the disturbance, Lorraine Harris would have seen me. But her mind wasn't on me. She looked preoccupied and grim. As she ran down the hall toward the trouble, her beautiful hair, knotted low on her neck, came loose. It made her look oddly girlish and vulnerable.

She had left open the door to the room she'd been in. I could see the screen of her computer. She hadn't had time to turn it off. I stepped closer. On the screen was a list of files. She had been deleting files, getting rid of evidence. Give us twenty-four hours, the note had said. Whatever these records were, they were important; I could use them as leverage to get Taylor. I tapped in the top code on the screen: spread sheets of financial records. Too complex. I tapped in the next code. More bookkeeping. I ran the list. Suddenly, I saw the code "teddy." The password Helmut Keating had told Jill to use to get into the Lily Pad computer.

The image of the teddy bear tattoo on Bernice Morin's left buttock flashed through my mind. Christy Sinclair had a teddy bear, too. I had seen it at the funeral home the night Mieka left me alone with Christy's body. The tattoos must have been a way of identifying the children as the property of the Lily Pad, a mark of possession like the brands burned into the flanks of cattle.

I typed the word *teddy*. Then I hit "Enter." The screen sprouted the kind of chart businesses use to explain their management structure. I recognized most of the names on the lower tiers: civic leaders in our towns and cities; politicians; two virulently homophobic ministers of God. The second name from the top was Lorraine Harris's. The top name was familiar, too: Con O'Malley, the president of NationTV. My boss. Jill had said the fax telling her to hire me as a panelist on *Canada Tonight* had come from his office.

O'Malley had covered all the bases. It wasn't hard to keep track of what I was doing from day to day. Lorraine was part of my family. And Jill was an employee of NationTV. When her investigation of the connection between Bernice Morin's death and the Little Flower murders hit pay dirt, Con O'Malley had bled her investigation dry by cutting off her money; then, when she persisted, he'd buried her in corporate busy work.

Busy work. That's what my job on the political panel had been. A distraction for a meddlesome woman. I looked at the management chart on the computer. Nothing was distracting me now. I hit the print key. In that quiet office, the printer seemed to roar to life, but I didn't have many options. The list had just finished printing when I felt a tug on the back of my slicker. I grabbed the gun in my pocket, and heart pounding, I turned. It was Taylor.

She was on the verge of tears, but she seemed all right. "I was beginning to get scared, Jo," she said. "Greg's mother said it was okay, but I was still getting scared."

I held her close to me. I could feel her heart beating against my chest. When I kissed the top of her head I could smell the warm, little-girl smell of her.

"No one hurt you, did they?"

She stood back, surprised. "Why would anybody hurt me?"

I ripped the sheet out of the printer and grabbed Taylor's hand. "Let's get out of here."

We started, then Taylor looked up at me. "I left my dolls," she said. She ran and picked up her candy box. By the time she came back, Lorraine Harris was standing at the door.

Lorraine was breathing hard, and there were darkening half-moons of sweat in the armpits of her cream jacket. But she was composed. Her oversized horn-rimmed glasses were lying on the table by the computer. She walked over, picked them up and put them on. It was a good look: the business-woman dealing with a crisis.

I stepped closer to her. "Hello, Lorraine," I said. "Going out of business?"

She looked quickly at the computer, at the printout in my hand, then at my face. For a time she was silent; I could almost hear the wheels turning as she decided which approach to take.

Finally, she made up her mind. "You can thank me that Taylor wasn't harmed," she said.

"Thank you?" I repeated, incredulous.

Taylor had heard her name and was looking at Lorraine with interest.

"The original plan was . . . different," Lorraine said.

There was a glassed-in space at the end of the room; it looked like a secretary's office. I pointed to it. "Taylor, why don't you go and sit in there till Lorraine and I are through talking. It'll be okay. You can see me, and I can see you."

Taylor went without question. She could feel the tension in the air.

As soon as Taylor closed the door to the office, Lorraine began to speak. Her voice was low, almost hypnotic. "The best thing for everybody would be if you just took Taylor and left. I give you my word that the business will be shut down. I'd already started to close things out. The decision came from Con O'Malley, Joanne. He won't go back on it. I'll be frank. The whole situation is just getting too hot – too many loose ends, too many people asking questions."

Her voice grew soft. "The Lily Pad is history, but our families aren't, are they? They're still making plans and thinking about the future. You have to protect them, Joanne. If you decide to be reasonable, no one will be hurt. Mieka's and Greg's wedding can be as perfect as you and I dreamed it would be. Keith's reputation won't be tarnished, and you'll have a brilliant future with the network. Sometimes, it's best just to walk away."

I felt myself being pulled into her orbit. Mieka had told me that Lorraine had taken courses in effective communication. She'd gotten her money's worth.

Lorraine touched my hand. "It will be as if the business never existed. I can erase everything."

"Including killing those girls," I said.

"I'm just management, Joanne. I don't kill anybody."

I felt laughter welling up in me. "You're just management?" I said.

"I never killed anybody," she said. "You have to believe me about that, Joanne. It wasn't me."

"Who was it, then?"

"Theresa. It was Theresa." Lorraine's grey eyes were the colour of winter ice. "They knew each other from before," she said. "Bernice had been at the Lily Pad when Theresa was in charge. Bernice was a difficult girl, a troublemaker; she didn't last. When she saw Theresa at Judgements that day, she threatened to tell Mieka the truth unless Theresa gave her money, a lot of money. Theresa panicked. She knew Bernice would keep asking for more. And she was desperately afraid Bernice would destroy her chance of being part of your family again." Lorraine covered my hand with her own. "In a way Theresa did it for you, Joanne."

I pulled my hand free of hers. "What happened to Theresa then?" I asked.

"She fell apart. She was terrified you'd find out the truth about her. And then when she saw me that night at the lake, she felt as if the walls were closing in. Of course, she knew I wouldn't expose her, but she told me it seemed as if all the ghosts of the past were rising up at once. I tried to help her. I offered to make arrangements so she could get away. I have connections."

I thought of the names on the computer print-out. They were men of power who were linked by a common sexual obsession; they were a brotherhood of pederasts.

"She could have pulled it off," Lorraine said. "She started, but she just seemed to lose her nerve. Killing Bernice did something to her. She'd tried to make what happened look like the Little Flower murders because she knew the cops don't push those investigations hard. But I think having to do it that way affected her. I'd known Theresa from the time she was ten years old, but I'd never seen her the way she was that night. She just didn't seem to have any resources left. I was going to help her. You have to believe that. But she found those pills in my bathroom and took them." Something animal and cunning flickered in her eyes. "I think she was afraid to face you, Joanne. I think she was afraid that if you found out the truth, you'd hate her."

"She killed herself because of me?" I said in a voice that didn't sound like mine. I felt myself losing ground.

"No one's without fault here," Lorraine said reasonably. "That's why it's best just to close things off without too many questions."

No one's without fault here. Her words seemed to resonate in me, touching hidden vulnerabilities. I thought of Peter. The possibility that Lorraine was right appeared at the edge of my mind. Perhaps it was best not to delve too deeply.

Then I remembered the other death. I moved closer to her. I could feel the pressure of Jackie's gun against my leg.

"And Kim Barilko?"

Lorraine twisted her hair back in a loop, then smiled at me, woman to woman. "I'll be frank, Jo. Helmut acted on his own initiative there, and he made a serious mistake. He thought it was a matter of security. He didn't know how much Theresa had told Kim and he didn't know how much Kim was about to tell you. It was a simple case of overreaction."

I knew she was lying. If Helmut had murdered Kim, he wouldn't be running from Con O'Malley and Lorraine, he'd be demanding that they protect him.

Lorraine cocked her head and gave me a winsome smile. "Don't overreact, Jo. Remember those pictures Mieka took? Remember all those shots of the two mothers addressing wedding invitations that she's saving for the grandchildren? Take Taylor back to the city now; I'll drive in tomorrow, and we can all just pick up where we left off."

I could see Lorraine's body relax. She thought she had me. She'd thought she could win, so she played her trump card. "Our kids need us," she said, and her voice was like honey. "Think of the children."

"I am," I said, sliding my hand into my pocket and curling my fingers around the handle of Jackie's gun. "I am thinking of the children. All of them. That's all I'm thinking about.

At the moment I'm thinking about the children you've got
locked up here. I want them. Jackie Desjarlais and I are going
to take them with us, and you're never going to touch them
again. Do you hear me? You're never going to violate another
child." My legs had started to shake, but my voice sounded
strong. It sounded like a voice Lorraine should listen to.

I pulled the gun out and pointed it at her. "Come on," I
said. "You and I are going to walk out of this room, and
you're going to tell the people who work for you to bring the
children to the dock. And Jackie and I are going to take them
out of this cesspool. If it takes two trips, I'll wait with them.
We're taking those children, and they're never coming
back." My voice was rising. "Do you hear me, Lorraine?
You're never going to sell another child again."

She looked at the gun, then she shrugged. "Have it your
way, Joanne. I've never known how to deal with self-righteous
women. You come in here like an avenging angel, sword in
hand, all set to smite me down. Well, smite the fuck away.
You won't be the first."

She took off her glasses and rubbed the bridge of her nose.
She looked weary and wounded. "Tell me, Joanne, how do
you think I got into this business? Do you think it was a
career option, like deciding between being a doctor and a
lawyer the way you and your friends did?"

"I don't want to hear this," I said.

Her mouth curled in derision. "Really? Well, I've decided
you should hear this, Mieka's middle-class mother. Do you
know how I met Con O'Malley? He bought me." She pointed
in the direction of Blue Heron Point. "Over there at the
Angler's Corner. My aunt was in there, drunk as usual,
broke as usual. When Con came in, she offered to sell me for
a bottle of beer. I was eleven years old." She looked hard at
me. "What were you doing when you were eleven, Joanne?
Dancing school? Pyjama parties with your friends? Con and

I had pyjama parties, till he decided I was too old. That was when he gave me a choice: go back to the Angler's Corner and be bought by anybody who had beer money or help him find some girls to replace me. Those were my career options, Joanne. Before you raise your sword, think about that. Think about how hard another woman had to work to make a good life for herself and her son. I'm not begging; I'm just asking for some consideration."

"I'll give you some consideration," I said, and I meant it. But as I walked through the Lily Pad, listening to Lorraine instruct her employees to bring the children to the docks, I kept Jackie's gun aimed at the back of her neck. No one gave me any trouble. Jackie was right. People were scared shitless of guns.

It took half an hour to get everybody down to the docks. There was a big cabin cruiser that belonged to the Lily Pad. Jackie was taking the children in that. We watched them climb on board. They were attractive and well dressed, but they seemed meek and spiritless. As they settled into their seats, I wondered if we'd been too late, if they were already beyond rescue. There were only seven of them, four girls and three boys. The woman who had cleaned off the tennis courts explained there had been a measles outbreak, and the others were quarantined in Blue Heron Point.

Two women whom Lorraine referred to as counsellors went in the boat with the children. The kids were afraid to be separated from them. Taylor and Lorraine and I were going to follow the cabin cruiser in Jackie's boat.

Finally, when everyone was in, Jackie turned and yelled to me. "Ready? I'll take it slow. Stay with me and you'll be fine."

I waved to him. Then a boy near the back of the cabin cruiser clambered over the seats to Jackie, leaned toward him and whispered something in his ear. Jackie nodded and the boy jumped out of the boat and ran to the Lily Pad. When he came back, Jackie gave me the high sign, and we began moving across the water.

Lorraine didn't speak on the trip back. Neither did Taylor. I was relieved. I didn't have any words left in me. I was grateful beyond measure that Taylor was sitting less than a metre away from me, bright and unharmed, but I had been running on adrenaline, and the adrenaline had stopped pumping. I was bone weary, and I was overwhelmed with the problems that lay ahead, what to do about Lorraine, and what would happen to the sad beaten children in the boat ahead.

As Blue Heron Point came into sight, I noticed there were people on the dock. We came closer and I saw that there were three of them. Keith was there, and Perry Kequahtooway, but the third figure was the one on whom my attention was riveted. As he recognized us in the boat, Blaine Harris raised his arm. It looked as if he was offering a benediction. I drove the boat parallel to the dock, helped Taylor out and handed the rope for mooring to Keith. Then I walked to where the old man waited in his wheelchair.

"You want to tell me something," I said.

"The rain. Killdeer," he said. Then he handed me a piece of newsprint, soft with age and handling. It was the picture of Christy Sinclair that the paper had printed at the top of her obituary. I looked at the picture, then I repeated his words.

"Lorraine killed her," I said. "Lorraine killed Christy Sinclair." His arm fell limp at his side, and he smiled at me. I looked at the boat. Lorraine was alone there; her body had folded in on itself in defeat. Perry Kequahtooway walked down the dock and held out a hand to her. He helped her out of the boat, then walked her over to a black sedan that was parked on the service road behind the shacks.

"It's over," I said to Blaine Harris, and he nodded.

Keith came and put his arm around me. I was still wearing the drab green slicker Jackie had given me. The weather had become even muggier, and the slicker acted like a sauna, trapping the hot, moist air against my T-shirt. I could feel it sticking to my skin. My runners and the ankles of my blue jeans were crusted with beach sand and muck from the island.

"Keith, I'm so dirty," I said, moving away from his arm.

"You look all right to me," he said, pulling me back. This time I didn't move away.

For a while I just stood there with his arm around me feeling tired. But I had to know. "Keith, what made you come up here?"

"My father."

"I have a friend who says Blaine's the most moral man she ever met."

Keith nodded. "He is that. I think that's why he's been going through such hell since that night at the lake. He saw something terrible happen, and he couldn't get anyone to understand what he'd seen."

I thought of the phone calls, the anguished words in the night.

Keith said, "Today when Dad and I were at the airport, waiting to get on the plane for Minneapolis, he showed me the picture of Christy he just gave you, and he tried those three words again: the rain killdeer. For the first time I put everything together. I started to ask Blaine questions. Had he seen Lorraine and Christy together that night? Had they quarrelled? Had he seen Lorraine do something to Christy? Maybe give her something to drink?" Keith sighed. "We were quite a pair: me badgering my father with all these questions, and Dad hooting away whenever I guessed right. Anyway, we did come up with a few things."

"Do you remember, Jo, that the room Dad was staying in out at the lake was Lorraine's room? The night Christy died, Dad's nurse had put him on the veranda outside the room to watch the sunset. The door to the inside was open, and Dad saw Lorraine come in and shake some kind of powder into a glass of whisky. When Christy came in, Lorraine gave her the drink. She probably told Christy it would calm her down. Christy drank the whisky. That's all we know for certain right now. But as far as I was concerned it was enough to call Perry Kequahtooway. He thought it was enough, too. That's why he came up with us."

Keith looked at the next dock. Jackie had tied up the cabin cruiser, and he and the women who worked for Lorraine were helping the children out of the boat.

"Jo, what the hell's going on here?" he asked.

I looked at this man whom I was beginning to love, and at his father, sitting in his wheelchair, looking at the lake, at peace for the first time in weeks.

"There's nothing going on that you have to know about now," I said. "It'll all be there tomorrow."

He looked at me hard. "It's bad, isn't it?"

I nodded.

"Then we should enjoy tonight," he said simply. "Are you and Taylor ready to come to the cottage?"

"The one with the squeaky screen door and the dishes that don't match and the wood box full of old *Saturday Nights*?" I said.

"The same," he said.

"My car is parked up there behind the shacks. Why don't you take Blaine up and get him settled?" I said. "I'll be right along, but there's some business I have to take care of. Could you give me five minutes?"

He smiled at me. "I told you before, Jo, I'm a patient man."

I took Taylor and we walked to the next dock and watched as Jackie made sure the big boat was safely moored. When he finished, he leaped out, graceful as a cat, and walked to the end of the dock. We followed him. The sun was dropping in the sky; as it fell, it made a path of light on the water. The fishermen's boats were heading toward shore. Time to come home.

It was Taylor who saw it first. She grabbed my hand and pointed. "Look," she said, "there's a fire over there, where we were."

At first, it was just a kind of heat shimmer in the sky above the channel, then the smoke began to rise, and the acrid smell of burning wood began to drift toward us. We watched in silence as the sky close to the water glowed red and then grew dark.

When the smoke thinned into fingers that seemed to reach into the sky, I touched Jackie's arm. "When that boy came over and talked to you in the boat before we left, what did he want?"

"Matches," Jackie said. "Matches so he could set his bed on fire."

"I'll take that drink now," I said.

The rye burned my throat, but it felt good. As I handed the bottle to Jackie, the sun glinted off the Wandering Soul bracelet. It was time. I slid the bracelet off and handed it to Jackie.

"I think she'd want you to have it," I said.

He touched the letters carefully with his forefinger, like a blind man reading Braille. Then he pulled his arm back and, in a graceful sweep, he skipped the bracelet across the water. For a heartbeat, it bounced along, flashing in the light from the dying sun; then it sank beneath the surface without a trace.

CHAPTER

13

I made one final trip to Lorraine's island. It was the morning after the fire. Taylor and I had spent the night at Keith's cabin. We had all been too tired for anything beyond bathing in the lake and collapsing into bed; sleep had come easily. The next morning, early, very early, Taylor woke me up. She'd been awakened by a scratching at the window. It was Jackie Desjarlais.

"I want to take you and Little Sister to breakfast," he whispered. "I've got something I need to talk to you about."

I looked into the bedroom with the twin beds; Keith and his father were still sleeping. Taylor, ready for adventure, had already pulled her shorts on. I wrote a note for Keith and slid it under the sugar bowl on the kitchen table, then I splashed water on my face, rinsed out my mouth and pulled on yesterday's clothes. Everything else was still in suitcases at the shacks.

We had breakfast at the café next to the hotel. When we got there, an old man was sitting on the porch watching two dogs fighting in the dirt out front. They were the same dogs who'd been fighting the day we arrived at Blue Heron Point.

When we left the restaurant, the old man was still there, and so were the dogs.

We walked down to the docks. For a while we just listened to the water lap the shore, then Jackie lit a cigarette and turned to me. "I'm going out there for a last look," he said. "I want to make sure there's nothing left of that fucker. You want to come along?"

"Yes," I said, "I think we do."

As we pushed off from land, it had seemed like a perfect day. The water was shimmering in the summer sunlight, and the sky was as cloudless and blue as the sky in the postcard Lorraine left when she abducted Taylor. But as we came through the narrows, the smell of wood smoke was heavy, and in the north a cloud, dense and malevolent, hung in the air above the island.

We moved slowly around the shoreline. We were, I think, stunned by the enormity of what had happened in the past twenty-four hours. The devastation was Biblical. The pines that had hidden the Lily Pad from prying eyes had been savaged by the fire. Stripped of needles and branches, they seemed spectral in the hazy air. The building was in ruins; nothing remained of it but a charred and smouldering skeleton. At the back, the steel door to the storage room hung crazily from its metal frame, guarding nothing. Flames had licked the playground equipment black, but it had survived, at least for a while. Unused, forgotten, it would rust and corrode; some day, in a hundred years, or a thousand, it would be gone, too.

"I can't believe that nobody even came out to the island to try to save it," I had said to Jackie as we headed back across the lake.

He had shrugged. "I think a lot of people in town were glad to see it burn. A lotta secrets in that building. A lotta things people want forgotten." Then he had turned to Taylor and smiled. "Come on, Little Sister. Time to learn how to drive a boat."

She moved to sit beside him. As she steered the boat across the shining lake, her face was flushed with pride. So was Jackie's. Once Theresa Desjarlais had taught her brother how to guide a boat through uncertain waters; now it was her brother's turn. As if he'd read my mind, Jackie Desjarlais looked up at me and yelled over the sound of the motor, "It all comes around, eh?"

"Yeah," I said, smiling back. "It all comes around."

Mieka and Greg were married in the chapel of St. Paul's Cathedral on Labour Day weekend. It was a small wedding. Hilda McCourt came down from Saskatoon, and Jill Osiowy was there to tape the ceremony for the mother who was not there. But these old friends aside, just Keith, Blaine and my children and I were sitting in the pews of that old and beautiful chapel.

In July, the papers had been filled with stories about Lorraine and Con O'Malley. At the beginning of August, the police solved the Little Flower case. When he realized that there would be no big payoff from NationTV, Darren Wolfe decided to become the police's star witness. His information was right on the money. The police moved quickly with their arrests, and the familiar picture of Con O'Malley touching the hibiscus in Lorraine's hair gave way to shots of four young pimps with smouldering eyes being escorted to and from their court appearances. As Tom Zaba had surmised, the Little Flower case was a simple matter of pimp justice. It lacked the cachet of the Harris-O'Malley case, but it pushed Lorraine's case to the back pages during the dog days of August, and we were grateful. Lorraine's story would, we knew, resurge when the trial began in early winter, but until then we all welcomed the protective cloak of a private wedding.

From the day Lorraine Harris was brought back from Blue Heron Point, Greg and Mieka had been her support and her comfort. Lorraine was being held at the correctional centre where Jill and I had visited Darren Wolfe, and Mieka and Greg hadn't missed a visiting day. They had no illusions about the horror of what she had done, but she was family, and for both of them, family was a link that was permanent.

Mieka and Greg's wedding day was a poignant one. They had learned early and publicly that marriage means caring for one another in good times and bad, and the knowledge had left its mark. As the summer sun poured through the stained-glass window, I leaned forward to look at my daughter. Under the filmy circle of her summer hat, Mieka's profile was as lovely and delicate as the face on a cameo, but there was sadness there, and there was sadness in the face of the man she loved.

The archdeacon's voice was solemn as he read from the Book of Alternative Services: "The union of man and woman in heart, body and mind is intended for their mutual comfort and help, that they may know each other with delight and tenderness in acts of love."

I thought of the seven children who had come back with us from the island to Blue Heron Point. Seven faces, pale, dead-eyed, not young, not old, not fearing, not hoping. They were in foster homes now, their futures dark and uncertain. And I thought of Bernice Morin, the veteran of the streets who believed in unicorns, and of Theresa Desjarlais standing in the field watching the tundra swans – "if they're smart and they're lucky, they'll make it" – and of Kim Barilko, her expression flickering between longing and contempt as she looked through the glass at wedding dresses that would always be for others, never for her.

"Pray for the blessing of this marriage," said the archdeacon. Beside me, Hilda McCourt, magnificent in mauve, dropped to the kneeler like a teenager. After a moment, I knelt, too. I prayed for Greg and Mieka, that their marriage would be a good one and that their lives would be happy. And then, as I had every morning that summer, I prayed for the wandering souls.

If you enjoyed

THE
WANDERING
SOUL
MURDERS

treat yourself to all of the
Joanne Kilbourn mysteries,
now available in stunning new
trade paperback editions
and as eBooks

McCLELLAND & STEWART

www.mcclelland.com
www.mysterybooks.ca

DEADLY APPEARANCES

When Andy Boychuk drops dead at a political picnic, the evidence points to his wife. Joanne takes her first "case" as Canada's favourite amateur sleuth as she seeks to clear Eve Boychuk, discovering along the way a Bible college that isn't all it seems. . . .

"A compelling novel infused with a subtext that's both inventive and diabolical." – Montreal *Gazette*

Trade Paperback 978-0-7710-1324-9   Ebook 978-0-7710-1322-5

MURDER AT THE MENDEL

"TENSE, MASTERFULLY WRITTEN. . . . BOLD AND POWERFUL."
– PUBLISHERS WEEKLY

Joanne's childhood friend, Sally Love, is an artist who courts controversy. When Sally's former partner turns up dead, Joanne discovers the past they shared was much more complicated, sordid, and deadly than she ever guessed.

"Classic. . . . Enough twists to qualify as a page turner. . . . Bowen and her genteel sleuth are here to stay." – Saskatoon *StarPhoenix*

Trade Paperback 978-0-7710-1321-8   Ebook 978-0-7710-1320-1

THE WANDERING SOUL MURDERS

"BOWEN GETS BETTER WITH EACH FORAY."
– EDMONTON JOURNAL

Joanne's peace is destroyed when her daughter finds a young woman's body near her shop. The next day, her son's girlfriend drowns, an apparent suicide. When it is discovered that the two young women had at least one thing in common, Joanne is drawn into a twilight world where money can buy anything.

"With her rare talent for plumbing emotional pain, Bowen makes you feel the shock of murder." – *Kirkus Reviews*

Trade Paperback 978-0-7710-1319-5   Ebook 978-0-7710-1318-8

A COLDER KIND OF DEATH

When the man convicted of murdering her husband six years earlier is himself shot, Joanne is forced to relive the most horrible time of her life. But it soon gets much worse when the prisoner's menacing wife is found dead a few nights later, strangled with Joanne's own silk scarf . . .

"A terrific story with a slick twist at the end."
– *Globe and Mail*

Trade Paperback 978-0-7710-1317-1   Ebook 978-0-7710-1316-4

A KILLING SPRING

The head of the School of Journalism at Joanne's university is found in a seedy rooming house wearing only women's lingerie and an electrical cord around his neck. When other events indicate that it was not a case of accidental suicide, Joanne finds herself deep in a world of fear, deceit, and danger.

"A compelling novel as well as a gripping mystery."
– *Publishers Weekly*

Trade Paperback 978-0-7710-1315-7   Ebook 978-1-5519-9613-4

VERDICT IN BLOOD

The corpse of the respected — and feared — Judge Justine Blackwell is found in a Regina park. Joanne tries to help a good friend involved in a struggle over which of Blackwell's wills is valid, and those who stand to lose the inheritance may well be murderers willing to strike again.

"An entirely satisfying example of why Gail Bowen has become one of the best mystery writers in the country."
– *London Free Press*

Trade Paperback 978-0-7710-1311-9   Ebook 978-1-5519-9614-1

BURYING ARIEL

Ariel Warren, a young colleague at Joanne's university, is stabbed to death in the library, and two men are under suspicion. The apparently tight-knit academic community is bitterly divided, vengeance is in the air, and Joanne is desperate to keep the wrong person from being punished for Ariel's death.

"Nearly flawless plotting, characterization, and writing." – *London Free Press*

Trade Paperback 978-0-7710-1309-6   Ebook 978-1-5519-9615-8

THE GLASS COFFIN

Joanne's friend Jill is about to marry a celebrated documentary filmmaker, both of whose previous wives committed suicide – after he had made films about them. When the best man's dead body is found just hours before the ceremony, Joanne begins to truly fear for her friend's safety.

"Chilling and unexpected." – *Globe and Mail*

Trade Paperback 978-0-7710-1305-8   Ebook 978-1-5519-9616-5

THE LAST GOOD DAY

Joanne is on holiday at a cottage in an exclusive enclave owned by lawyers from the same prestigious firm. When one of them kills himself the night after a long talk with Joanne, she is pushed into an investigation that has startling – and possibly fatal – consequences.

"A classic whodunit in which everything from setting to plot to character works beautifully. . . . A treat from first page to final paragraph." – *Globe and Mail*

Trade Paperback 978-0-7710-1349-2   Ebook 978-1-5519-9617-2

THE ENDLESS KNOT

After journalist Kathryn Morrissey publishes a tell-all book on the adult children of Canadian celebrities, one of the parents angrily confronts her and as a result is charged with attempted murder. When the parent hires Zack Shreve, the new love in Joanne's life, to defend him, her own understanding of the knot that binds parent and child becomes both personal and very urgent.

"A late-night page turner.... A rich and satisfying read." – *Edmonton Journal*

Trade Paperback 978-0-7710-1347-8   Ebook 978-1-5519-9246-4

THE BRUTAL HEART

A local call girl is dead, and her impressive client list includes the name of Joanne's new husband. Shaken that Zack saw the woman regularly before they met, Joanne throws herself into her work and is soon embroiled in a bitter and increasingly strange custody battle of a local MP, who is simultaneously trying to win an election.

"Elegant.... Joanne rules the narrative. [*The Brutal Heart*] slips along with grace and style." – *Toronto Star*

Trade Paperback 978-0-7710-0994-5   Ebook 978-1-5519-9233-4

THE NESTING DOLLS

Just before she is murdered, a young woman hands her baby to a perfect stranger and disappears. The stranger is the daughter of lawyer Delia Wainberg, and soon a secret from Delia's youth comes out. Not only is a killer on the loose, but the dead woman's partner is demanding custody of the child, and the battle threatens to tear apart Joanne's own family.

"The underlying human drama of love and good intentions gone very, very bad make the novel a compelling read." – *Vancouver Sun*

Trade Paperback 978-0-7710-1276-1   Ebook 978-0-7710-1277-8

Edward Willet

GAIL BOWEN's first Joanne Kilbourn mystery, *Deadly Appearances* (1990), was nominated for the W.H. Smith/ Books in Canada Best First Novel Award. It was followed by *Murder at the Mendel* (1991), *The Wandering Soul Murders* (1992), *A Colder Kind of Death* (1994) (which won an Arthur Ellis Award for best crime novel), *A Killing Spring* (1996), *Verdict in Blood* (1998), *Burying Ariel* (2000), *The Glass Coffin* (2002), *The Last Good Day* (2004), *The Endless Knot* (2006), *The Brutal Heart* (2008), and *The Nesting Dolls* (2010). In 2008 *Reader's Digest* named Bowen Canada's Best Mystery Novelist; in 2009 she received the Derrick Murdoch Award from the Crime Writers of Canada. Bowen has also written plays that have been produced across Canada and on CBC Radio. Now retired from teaching at First Nations University of Canada, Gail Bowen lives in Regina. Please visit the author at www.gailbowen.com.